The Wind's Story

The Wind's Story

Anne B. Udy

Library of Congress Control Number: 2015919588
ISBN: Hardcover 978-1-5144-4319-4
Softcover 978-1-5144-4320-0
eBook 978-1-5144-4321-7

This is a work of fiction. Names, characters, places and incidents either are the product of the author's imagination or are used fictitiously, and any resemblance to any actual persons, living or dead, events, or locales is entirely coincidental.

Print information available on the last page.

Rev. date: 11/30/2015

To order additional copies of this book, contact:
Xlibris
1-800-455-039
www.Xlibris.com.au
Orders@Xlibris.com.au
728556

Dedicated to my parents,
William Ellsbury Benua and Emily Platt Benua who
filled my childhood with poems and stories.

"The invisible wind's utterance amid unseen things..."

-Eden Phillpotts

Chapter 1

Grandmothers' tales, as our mother called them, are the 'ones told by the wind as it blew across the land and the river—rustling the leaves, bending the young trees, vibrating the bushes, making the tall grasses bow and the water skip and splash'.

Once, long ago—as the tales related—there were two kingdoms west of reality, east of wherever you are and so small that cartographers forgot to put them on their maps. Both Riparia and the Land of Far lay almost unnoticed by the large countries which surrounded them.

Riparia was named for its most prominent feature, the river which bisected it. It was shaped like a violin, with the northern third a long thin strip—not much wider than the river until the land widened suddenly into an almost hourglass shape. The only city, Aviol, sat in the middle of the widened section with a bridge more or less at the spot where it would have been on a musical instrument.

Next to Riparia in the north-west and separated from it by a sheer and immense cliff was the Land of Far, a mountain kingdom covered in deep snow for ten months of the year.

One of the grandmothers' tales told to me by my own grandmother began with a child who lived in the royal palace of Riparia. She was the daughter of the royal housekeeper, and her name was Amethyst. She had long black hair, grey-green eyes which were generally sparkling, and a straight middle-sized nose which turned down at the end. She and her mother, Sylvia, had a pleasant flat in 'the backstairs wing'—the palace servants' area. From their flat, they had a grand view across the kitchen gardens to an area of large houses surrounded by trees. But for Amethyst, the royal corridor was the best and most exciting place to be; she loved it when her mother had a job there and let her go along.

The royal corridor led to the royal apartments as well as the throne room, the banquet hall, the royal library, and a small meeting room where the king met with his council. That was all of small interest; it was the corridor itself which fascinated her.

Here Amethyst imagined herself in the rich clothing and jewellery of the ladies whose portraits hung in elaborate gold frames. Beneath the portraits, glass-fronted cabinets held such wonders as miniature ships and animals made from ivory, wood, and jewels. There was a whole doll's house with all the trimmings: carpet, curtains, furniture, kitchen equipment, people, and even a dog, cat, and pony.

She would wander slowly along the corridor, delighting in the colours and shapes. By the time her mother had finished checking on the cleaning a new maid had done and had arranged the flower displays to her satisfaction, Amethyst would be lost in a sea of ideas and possibilities. She was never prepared for the shock of being told it was time to leave.

One day her mother paused long enough to point out a polished purple stone. 'That's your stone, my darling, an amethyst.'

So that was the source of her name. She was thrilled. What a beautiful colour, so clear and peaceful. Would she—could she ever have a stone of her very own?

'Could it really be mine', she asked her mother, 'to hold in my hand, to keep?'

Sylvia doubted it, but she said, 'Study and work hard, my darling. If you get a tutoring job with a wealthy family, who knows what you might own?'

Amethyst was a bright child, curious about everything. There was no school for servants' children, but her father had been a teacher, and Sylvia was determined that their daughter would learn to read, write, and speak properly. Sylvia did not plan for her to be a housekeeper. Every day she assigned sums to do, paragraphs and then pages to write, and books to read. She tested her on all of it. Sylvia also taught her housekeeping skills; at an early age, Amethyst took over most of the care of their flat.

As head royal housekeeper, Sylvia had some contact with Queen Florence, who took a real interest in the families of the servants she encountered—in contrast to King Marco, for whom servants were people whose sole purpose was to serve. The queen had come from far away; one of her ways of managing her frequent times of sadness was to involve herself in helping others.

When she heard about Sylvia's desire to educate her daughter, she offered to lend her books. She was especially kind to Sylvia because she felt she understood the housekeeper's desire to encourage Amethyst to become something more than what might have been her normal lot. The queen too had a child, Prince Rio, whom she was anxious to influence to be more concerned with the welfare of others than her husband, the king, appeared to be.

The prince was only about a year older than Amethyst, so when he and his tutor had finished with each year's texts and workbooks, they were passed on to Amethyst. When the queen gave Amethyst a book from the royal library, it became her most treasured possession.

Few of the other servants' children could read or write, but Amethyst liked playing games or just relaxing with them. She had to be careful not to use their speech when she was with her mother, although she was quite good at copying it when she was with them. However, she was not allowed to join them until she finished all her set work. This was only one of the motivations that had pushed her to learn and learn and to do it without wasting time. She was also an eager reader. It only took her half the time her mother expected before she was free to go. The other children warmly welcomed the girl with the round smiling face and the wonderful stories. The small ones vied to hold her hand or climb on to her lap.

Prince Rio was thirteen when the king hired a new tutor for him. Professor Chen was highly recommended, having just achieved his professorship at the early age of twenty-five. The king was delighted to hire such a notable younger man who expressed due regard for the honour being conferred on him as well as excitement at the challenge of the job. At the queen's suggestion, he was also to spend an hour five days a week teaching the children of the palace servants to read, write, and gain some knowledge of simple arithmetic.

After his first week, the tutor asked for a meeting with the king. He was shown to the royal library, where both royal parents welcomed him. The queen was the first to speak, 'I am delighted to meet you, Professor. I believe you are challenging my son in new ways.'

'I believe in challenge, Your Majesty, and His Highness is one of the subjects I wished to discuss with you.'

'Oh, is that so?' the king put in. 'You find him unsatisfactory in some respect?'

'To my way of thinking, it is only Your Majesties who can pass a judgement on what is satisfactory or unsatisfactory in this situation.'

The king spoke again, 'So what have you to report?'

'His Highness, Prince Rio, is extremely bright. Like many bright children, he can learn enough to get by very well without effort. He's bored with his schoolwork. Yet he does not want to rise to challenges I have tried. It seems to me he needs something to retrigger a delight in learning and discovery.'

'Do you have a suggestion?' the queen asked.

'Indeed, Your Majesty, I have. There is a twelve-year-old girl among the servants' children who is totally beyond the others. In fact, it appears to me that she may be on par with the prince. She also is exceptionally intelligent but fully engaged in learning. It seems that to her studying is a pleasure, an exciting opportunity. There is no point in her coming to the class with the others. However, it seems to me that if she were to study with His Highness, it could awaken his interest. Also, competition with another student might be just what he needs.'

The king made a noise in his throat rather like a harrumph and frowned.

'Amethyst is all you say, Professor,' replied the queen. 'Unlike the other children, she speaks well and has had the use of our son's old texts and study guides for some years.'

'I didn't know that,' remarked the king, still frowning. 'But she's a servant's child. Study with the prince? I don't think so. I can't imagine why you let her have the books.'

The queen did not respond to her husband but to the tutor. 'We'll think about it, Professor, and let you know. Thank you so much for giving us your suggestion.'

The tutor left them to make their decision.

On the first morning Amethyst was to join Prince Rio, Sylvia fussed over her. 'You've missed a spot on your left shoe. Let me have that comb. Be sure to stand up straight and speak respectfully.'

The girl hardly heard her. She wondered whether life as the child of one of the royal servants was more difficult than that of the king's son. Surely the queen was not at this moment treating her son like a prized sculpture just about to go on display.

Her mother continued the monologue. 'This is an opportunity of a lifetime. You will be the envy of every girl in Riparia.'

Amethyst wasn't sure about that. She would have traded places with *any* other girl in the kingdom. She was happy with things as they had been, but now she was being asked to spend her mornings studying with the prince, who looked like a spoiled and stuck-up snob when he appeared in an overdecorated uniform with his parents on state occasions. She was to get him interested in his lessons if only because he did not want to be beaten by another student. It felt like the end of enjoying studying, reading, and playing—of being in charge of her own life.

When it was time, her mother took her through the palace corridors to the servants' doorway leading into the royal gardens, where the tutor had his cottage. 'You're on your own now. Make me proud of you.'

Amethyst heard the door close behind her. She stood, taking deep breaths and trying to still the shaking in her body. She considered going back into the palace and hiding in her bedroom, but she lifted her head, swung her long black hair from side to side a couple of times and moved reluctantly along the garden walk.

Before she saw the cottage, the prince appeared—bouncing towards her. Quickly he was close enough for her to see his encompassing smile. He was more handsome than she had thought him when she had seen him from a distance. He was taller than she was, with slightly curly mid-brown hair.

'Welcome, Amethyst,' he began, then grabbed her as she overbalanced, tripping herself up in her confusion. He held on to her hand as she steadied herself.

'O . . . O, Your Highness,' she gasped as her face got redder and redder.

'I'm Rio, for the river, you know. I'll call you Amethyst. You call me Rio.'

She didn't know what to say and was glad when he let go of her hand. How annoyed her mother would be if she knew how badly her daughter had begun.

Rio chatted on as if all was well. He'd gone to meet her in case she did not know the way to the tutor's cottage. But she was hardly aware of anything except her blunder. Before she could recover, he was helping her up the stairs of the cottage, and they entered their schoolroom.

'I bring you your new pupil, Professor Chen.' Then he turned to the girl. 'This is Professor Chen, our tutor.'

Amethyst did not take in the details of the schoolroom—bookshelves which almost surrounded them, the tutor's large desk in front, the two windows, or the few pictures on the walls.

She would have been glad to drop through a hole in the floor, but the professor took her arm, settled her into a chair at one of the two student desks, and brought her a glass of water.

Professor Chen began gently, asking questions about things he was sure they would know. Amethyst would have kept quiet and let the prince answer every time, but the questions were directed alternately to the prince and then to her. She was beginning to relax, but she kept her eyes averted, only looking up at the tutor when he spoke her name. When he set them work to do, she finished well ahead of the prince. It embarrassed her, but she liked the compliments from Professor Chen and Prince Rio.

About every hour, the tutor got them up and all three did stretches or took a brisk walk in the gardens. Amethyst was a bundle of smiles in the garden. When she had first entered, she had noticed nothing, but now she looked eagerly in every direction and longed to know the names of all the flowers, bushes, and trees. She was delighted when the prince offered to help her pick a bouquet on her way home.

So she returned to her part of the palace with her bouquet and a wide smile. But she lost her smile at 'I hope you always addressed the prince by his proper title'. Her mother wanted to know details, especially about manners and behaviour. She did not want to know about the garden or if the time had been enjoyable or even what subjects they covered. Amethyst found she had little to tell. However, she no longer thought her enjoyment of studying was at an end.

The prince reported to his mother that he was unable to keep up with his new fellow student. She was delighted. 'I thought that girl would shake you up a bit.'

Soon Amethyst looked forward to finding Rio's oval face, with its brown eyes and slightly turned-up nose, smiling at her when she entered the garden. She was also relaxed with Professor Chen, but she was puzzled about him. He reminded her of the Japanese undercook in the royal kitchen, but when she studied his face, she could not discover what was oriental about it. He did dress in loose trousers and wore a short kimono-type jacket with a sash, but was that all there was to it?

Amethyst found it was fun studying with a companion—especially when the prince quickly caught up with her and was in the lead about half the time. Both students thrived on the competition. In the schoolroom, they concentrated on their lessons, but at breaks in the garden, Rio was apt to shout, 'I will beat you to the pergola' or 'I will be the first one to do twelve push-ups.' In both cases, he was correct, but Amethyst was improving.

The prince always entered the garden directly from the royal apartments but took to waiting at the servants' door for Amethyst. He would tell her the names of the plants and stories of the people who had planned and made the wandering pathways with secluded areas for benches and a pergola.

Sometimes he organised a picnic. The two students and the professor would sit under the pergola, eating chicken, tiny bread-and-butter sandwiches, and fruit from the royal orchard. The three of them developed a close relationship, almost a feeling of family.

The friendship of the prince and Amethyst was noted by the king and queen. The queen saw no harm in it and appreciated the difference it had made to the prince's studies. The king did not express an objection. Amethyst herself was still afraid her knees would collapse under her if she happened to see Rio's parents.

The first sign of a real problem came when the prince turned eighteen, and a grand ball to celebrate the occasion was planned. The king sent for him. 'You will, of course, dance with many different ladies during the evening. However, you may choose one to escort and sit with at the banquet.'

'Amethyst, of course,' replied the prince.

'Never.' The king scowled at his son. 'Sit down, Rio.'

The prince perched on the edge of a chair and looked at his father.

'It appears', said the king, 'that you are unaware of certain proprieties. You are a royal prince. You can, in certain prescribed instances, speak with those of inferior status, but they cannot be your friends and associates. A ball is for people of our own kind.'

'Amethyst is hardly inferior, Father—' Rio began, but King Marco silenced him with a snarl and a sharp slap on his son's arm.

'We will have no more of this sort of talk,' he almost shouted. 'That servant's child should never have been allowed to be tutored with you. Leave the room and keep away from her.'

Nothing more was said that day about the matter, but the next day, Rio was sent for again. This time, the queen was with her husband. She was the spokesperson. 'Rio, you have upset your father greatly, but I have explained to him that your mention of Amethyst in regard to your birthday ball was, of course, a joke. It's too bad he took it so seriously, but—'

'Mother, I was serious.'

'Stop it right now. It had better be a joke, even though it's a bad one. Use your brain, boy, and don't let us hear any more of such foolishness.'

The queen said they had chosen a distant cousin for him to escort. 'It will be a very happy and gala occasion. Thank you for coming. You may go now.'

The ball was organised in the established royal manner. Amethyst was to work in the kitchen as extra help would be needed.

* * *

On that same day, there was an event which Amethyst would never forget. It began with a tremendous bang on the apartment door. She felt the floor shake.

'Open in the name of the king' sounded around the corridors and through every room of the flat. Amethyst felt bolted to the couch, but her mother opened the door.

A thin bearded soldier, surely the tallest and fiercest Amethyst had ever seen, entered the room. He was dressed in the king's livery with a wide black sash over his left shoulder. He handed her mother a letter and commanded her to open it.

Visibly shaking, she pulled out a piece of paper, and her eyes traced the lines of writing.

'Read it out loud to your daughter.' He sounded to Amethyst like someone announcing the guillotine list for the day.

Sylvia found it hard to begin.

'Read.'

She began, but Amethyst could hardly hear her. 'Louder or give it to me.'

'To the royal house . . . keeper . . . and mother of . . . Amethyst . . .' Her mother wiped her eyes with the back of her hand.

The soldier reached for the letter, but her mother kept hold of it and went on more strongly, 'His Majesty, King Marco of Riparia, herewith informs you that His Royal Highness, Prince Rio, has shown friendship to your daughter—who has taken advantage of his kindness.' She glanced up at her daughter but read on. 'Amethyst will immediately join the trainee maids under your supervision and then be given a full-time job on the housekeeping staff. She may no longer attend classes with Prince Rio or have anything further to do with him . . .' She took a breath, but as the soldier moved towards her, she continued, 'As long as it does not interfere with her regular housekeeping duties, she may continue her studies in her spare time but may only consult Professor Chen once a week in the evening at his cottage. At no other time may she enter the royal gardens.'

When she paused again, the soldier grabbed the paper from her. 'Failure to comply with these directions will mean that both you and your daughter may both be prohibited from living in the royal palace or entering it at any time. Signed by His Majesty, King Marco of Riparia.'

The soldier handed the letter back to Sylvia, banged on the floor with his staff, made a stiff military about-face, and left.

Her mother closed the door, but Amethyst did not move. She did not speak. She felt hollow. There was nothing inside her and no future for her.

She understood. She had always known in a part of her mind that the dream in which she had been floating—a future shared with Rio—was a misty fairy tale that could not last. But now she knew it would be hard to get up in the morning. Actually, she did not even want to get off the couch.

* * *

The prince—although also instructed to have no more to do with her—made many attempts to find her. He refused to accept their separation. He was also convinced that his father would never expel Sylvia from the palace. She was too valuable a housekeeper. One day Amethyst was startled to find him in the royal library, which she had been sent to clean.

'Excuse me, Your Highness, I will . . .'

'Amethyst, what do you mean? I'm Rio.' He sprang up from his seat. He stood, blocking her way—not touching her. They stared into each other's eyes without speaking. The prince indicated she should occupy the seat he had vacated.

'O . . . Ah . . . No, Your Highness. I have . . . work to do.'

'Amethyst, don't you know me any more? Speak to me.'

'I cannot . . . I am not—O.' She slipped past him and ran, disappearing through the door through which she had entered.

But the prince was not easily deterred. He went to his father and demanded to have the prohibition reversed. He was given a firm response. She was, no doubt, an intelligent girl but not of a family with which the prince could have any relationship. She and her mother had been informed. There could be no connection between them.

The king also told his son that they were presently looking for ladies with the correct background who were available. The prince would have a chance to meet a number of them and choose a wife.

'I've already chosen Amethyst.'

'She's been a companion for your studies, but she is not someone who could ever become queen.'

'Why not? She'd make a great queen—intelligent, kind, beautiful . . .'

'Rio, you are a prince. She is a servant. I will hear no more of this.'

'And I refuse to meet any of your "available" ladies.' He turned and stumbled out of the room.

He did, in fact, end up attending balls and weeks of parties and activities. He met many beautiful women and was always polite. He was particularly kind to the shyest of his guests. Most of them fell in love with him.

The king and the queen were not aware that he always strolled in the garden at the time when Amethyst finished her lessons with the tutor and that Rio was still trying to convince her that they had a future together. He was determined that she was the woman he would marry. Of course, at the moment, his father had final say, but that would not always be the case. He had his own plans.

Chapter 2

When Rio was a child, the king's mother had lived in a ground-floor apartment which opened directly on to a secluded section of the royal gardens. Since her death, it was only used for occasional visitors. Rio began its redecoration after his twentieth birthday with the approval of his parents, who thought it natural that he would want his own space.

The apartment was nearly ready when the king took his son on a tour of royal palaces so that Rio could meet foreign princesses and peeresses.

While they were gone, Amethyst looked hard at her situation. She was exhausted by the inner struggle—a war, really—between her two selves. One looked forward to their continued meetings and the prince's assurance of a happy-ever-after conclusion. Her other self grew stronger. She knew his father would never consent to their marriage. In all likelihood, both she and Rio would be past middle age by the time he became king. It seemed to her she must act for both their sakes and even for the good of the country.

She made her decision.

The night the tour was to end was also the night for her lesson with Professor Chen. It must be her last visit to the garden which filled her life with such joy and her last lesson with the tutor whom she had come to love as a father. Hardest of all, it must be the end to all the ridiculous wishes, and even hopes, which had filled her thoughts and days for so long.

It was impossible. They must separate completely, live their lives so that they never met, spend their time with other people—or probably in her case, spend it alone. At the moment, she did not see how she could leave the palace, but she could stay out of the areas where they might meet. She would ask her mother to transfer her to the kitchen; she would tell the tutor tonight that there would be no more lessons for her. She would ask him to speak to Rio and inform the prince that he must not try to see her; he must stay in the royal areas and make no attempt to contact her.

Her feet were so heavy she could hardly move forward. Each step took too much strength. She got through the door and stood looking at the garden. She blinked. There was a man coming towards her. It was not her imagination, and it was not Rio. It was Professor Chen.

'Good evening, Amethyst. We have a different room for our lesson tonight.'

She did not reply, but he took her arm and led her down a narrow path to a door she had not seen before. He opened it for her, and when she just stood and looked, he took her arm again. They went through a short hallway and into a room full of light and colour where the prince stood waiting with a grin.

Amethyst stiffened, removed her arm from her escort, and turned to go. When Rio grabbed her and encircled her with his arms, she burst into tears.

The two men were at a loss. They got her seated on a couch, supplied her with handkerchiefs and a glass of water.

Her sobbing died down as she gained control. She sipped the water for a bit, then set it down. She gulped air; her body shook. Rio brought a blanket and wrapped it around her. When he sat beside her, she made a small shift away from him.

They sat in silence until an owl hooted in the tree by the front door. It seemed to wake Amethyst. She thought it was telling her she must speak.

Her voice was soft but clear. 'It . . . won't . . . work.' She disengaged her arms from the blanket and placed her hands gently on Rio's chest, holding him away. 'It is impossible.' He started to speak but stopped at a gesture from Professor Chen.

Amethyst sat up straighter. 'If only you were not a prince . . . or I was not . . .' She sighed.

Rio could hold back no longer. 'I will make you a queen.'

She faced him, and her voice strengthened. 'No, Rio. We come from different worlds . . . too far apart. We were not meant . . . to meet.' She leaned further away from him, against the soft cushions.

'Amethyst.' The prince's voice was almost a wail. 'We have met. I have prepared this home for you. I love you.'

She dropped her hands. 'Yes. I love you too. But a prince cannot marry a housemaid. A servant marries'—she gulped for breath—'a servant and a prince a princess. When I've worked out how to get a job . . . outside the palace, I'll be out of sight . . . not trouble you any more.'

'I want you to trouble me forever.' Rio had re-found his strong voice. 'I cannot live a life without you. You are wrong. We can marry, just not for a while. When I am king, I will approve our marriage, and all our children will be princes and princesses.'

For a moment, Amethyst's eyes went as wide as they could go, and her lips were parted. Then she closed her eyes and whispered, 'Please, oh please, Rio, no more. We cannot live on dreams forever.'

'You're right. Come today and live here with me.'

'I will not be your mistress,' she told him angrily. With regained strength, she rose to leave.

The prince fell on his knees in front of her. 'No, Amethyst, no. That is not what I want. My darling Amethyst, we will say vows to each other and be married in our hearts and minds. You will be my wife. When the king sees I am determined, he may consent. We will live here in the palace—together. Oh, my love.'

Amethyst looked at the prince, then at Professor Chen. He moved forward and took her arm. 'Rio, I think this lady has had all she can take for today. I will walk her home, but the two of you must meet again.'

Rio's whole body sagged as he watched them walk out of sight.

Perhaps she could stop thinking and let Professor Chen lead her, as he was doing now. Pain and confusion were still there, but it felt as though he was helping her to carry them.

They entered the building and walked through long hallways. 'Let it go for tonight, Amethyst. I know it's not finished . . .' They kept walking until they reached the stairway. Then he looked at her. 'Would you be willing to come with me to my sister's home?'

'How? Why?'

'I'm not sure.' He paused. 'She might need help with her housekeeping or . . .' His forehead wrinkled, and his eyes were almost shut. It was what Amethyst called his *heavy-thinking* face. It cleared the way the sun shines through a cloud. 'I need help with my book. That's it! Will you go with me to my sister's house and help?'

'Of course, Professor Chen, if I can. But I don't see—'

'You don't need to see. If I get it sorted out, just go along with it.'

They climbed the stairs. When her mother came to the door, the tutor sent Amethyst off to bed and asked for a word with Sylvia.

* * *

In the morning, her mother was agitated. 'I don't know about this plan of the professor's. What's going on, Amethyst?'

'What?'

'Professor Chen's asked me to organise time off for you to help him with some book he's writing—wants to take you away downriver somewhere. All this because I let him tutor you, and with the prince. It's made you strange, Amethyst, uppity, thinking you can—'

'Mother, stop it. What does Professor Chen want?'

'To take you to some house, his sister's, he said, and get your help . . . researching, transcribing. The king has ordered you to be a housemaid, and I think—'

Amethyst stood. 'I'm going out now and be a housemaid. See you later.' She closed the door behind her, stood staring into space for a couple of moments, and then went down to start her duties for the day.

* * *

The palace, once a place where Amethyst found interest and delight, had become for her almost a prison due to her strain and struggle within, her mother's attitude, and hostility—following the king's pronouncement—from those with whom she worked. There was no joy or peace there for her. Now she and Professor Chen had left through the front gates. There was more joy and even peace in the hustle and bustle outside the grounds, and she was determined to immerse herself in it. She focussed on her surroundings. The crowds jostled in all directions, laughing, shouting, chattering. The shopfronts were full of colour. This was a different world, and she could be part of it—at least for a while. She would enjoy every minute as much as possible.

Amethyst's eyes roamed, and Professor Chen held her arm in case she stumbled. Except for a few ohs, she did not speak. Her companion watched her and smiled.

They reached the wharf and saw the river. She had never seen this more-navigable section flowing to the south. She stopped suddenly and was nearly run into by the woman behind her.

'The river, it's so big. I never thought . . .' She took a big breath of the strange air with the smells of fish and grease mingled with scents of people, closely packed. 'Is that the boat? Is that it?'

They moved on to the pier. Bags were being loaded and a ramp put in place. When they boarded, the professor was known to the boatmen, who called out, 'How be y're sister? Y'll get off by her?'

They found seats near the bow. Amethyst watched the city disappear; farms and heavily treed areas took over.

'There's so much space, like the palace gardens stretched out and out. The little houses. See, look, horses and cows. Oh, Professor, is this real?'

Soon the ferry pulled towards a small dock. A dark-skinned man appeared. He had a limp, but he moved quickly, caught and secured the ropes, and helped settle the ramp. Their bags were offloaded before Amethyst and the professor stepped ashore.

'Jerry,' Professor Chen greeted him. 'This is one of my pupils, Amethyst. Amethyst, meet Jerry, the cleverest man I know for fixing anything.'

Jerry shook the professor's hand but did not speak. When he turned towards Amethyst, she thought the gleaming smile on his dark face was more welcoming than any words he could have said. They started towards the house. It was a cream building with two storeys. A couple of slender pillars stood by the four steps leading to a veranda and an open door. Hydrangea bushes bloomed in front.

As they walked forward, a woman appeared on the veranda. She was thin—too thin—and her full-length kaftan, with misty blues and yellows swirling round strong vertical black lines, made her seem taller than she was.

She spoke as they reached the steps. 'Welcome, Algernon and Algernon's student.' Her voice was not loud but scratchy. Amethyst looked up in amazement at the name she'd called her brother; the woman's eyes were not turned towards them. The woman did not look anything like her brother.

Professor Chen was up the steps and would have hugged his sister, but she shifted away. She looked at Amethyst. 'What do you intend to do with yourself, student of my brother?'

The professor answered, 'Amethyst's here to rest. She'll help with my book—not be in your way, Clotilde, not at all.'

The woman turned. The braid across her forehead continued around, the end hanging down at the back. They followed her into the house, where she disappeared.

A girl with Jerry's skin colour and smile appeared. 'Welcome, I'm Lou. There's tea in the next room.' She led them to a bright room overlooking a garden full of colour.

The professor reassured Amethyst, 'Don't let my sister worry you. She's not well. You won't see much of her.'

Inside, the house did not live up to its splendid location. For the most part, it was simply and just adequately furnished. There were few pictures on the walls, few trinkets in sight; rugs had been underfoot for many years, and a slight smell of mildew lingered.

However, in her room, the window was open, and the river smelled of fresh wet air with a faint reminder of fish that seemed to have blown anything else away.

* * *

It was a new experience to wake and not immediately get up. Amethyst stretched, yawned, rubbed her shoulders and arms, then curled back under the covers. After a bit, she got out of bed and went to the window. The river was still flowing. There was a sailboat making small progress against the current, but it was making progress. And so was she. She had washed and dressed before Lou came knocking with a cup of tea. After breakfast, she spent an hour proofreading for Professor Chen in his shed.

It was a plain wooden building. The main room had a wall of bookshelves, a huge flat desk with a straight-backed chair, and a smaller desk and a chair, where Amethyst was to work. There was also an area with a couch and three comfortable chairs. Several small windows let in light as did the door, which was usually open. Professor Chen did not stay in the house. The shed had a small bedroom. When he visited his sister, he could keep whatever hours he chose without troubling her.

After Amethyst helped the professor, the day was hers. Whatever she did, she could not forget the prince. She carried a heavy rock of loss, and much of her thinking was about the future. Maybe their tutor's sister could use an extra hand here, or perhaps she would know of someone who had need of a finely trained housekeeper.

Wandering through the house, she discovered a round old oak table with impressive claw feet surmounted by finely chiselled leaf motifs. Jerry found her oil to nourish the wood, and Lou supplied soft rags. She spent a long afternoon rubbing in the oil and polishing, making sure to rub every indentation or tiny crack.

The second day was similar. She even found a quaint glass-fronted curio cabinet in a cobwebbed corner. Dusting and polishing the cabinet and the few glass and ivory pieces inside it were a comforting accompaniment to her internal discussion of options. There was a prancing horse and a tiny house—in a snow storm when you turned it upside down. She thought of the royal corridor with its many curiosities and its grand doll's house. She would probably never see any of it again.

On the third and fourth days, she spent time in the library. She was dusting the books and making some small repairs to damaged covers. Her progress was extremely slow as there were many pauses when she could not deny herself the pleasure of reading pages and even chapters.

After the evening meal on the fourth day, the professor suggested a walk to the pier. Amethyst was watching the way the water bounced against it when he spoke, 'You will have a visitor tomorrow.' She looked up.

'Prince Rio is coming.'

Her eyes dropped back to watch the river. They both listened to its slap and pull against the posts of the pier.

'Is it too soon for you, Amethyst?'

She breathed deeply. 'No . . . but I hadn't thought . . .'

The river flowed on.

'You can see him privately . . . perhaps here, by the river. Or you can borrow my shed.'

'No, Professor. He is too . . . strong, too passionate.' She watched the river. 'You will be with me'—then more softly—'won't you?'

'I will, if you wish it.'

'Please.'

They moved back to the house. He put his hand on her shoulder before she entered. 'Sleep well, my child. Rio too has had time to think. You will decide together. You will not be overwhelmed.'

* * *

The next afternoon, a heavy sadness, barely touched by a ray of hope, held her firmly on the wooden bench above the river. Today she was looking for only one particular floating item. She watched the kayak turn across the current and dock below her. She could not turn her eyes from the figure which took the few steps with a bound. She barely managed to stand.

He stood in front of her. 'I am here, Amethyst. Do not run away.'

She was unable to speak.

Gently he turned her from the river, and she led him slowly past the house to Professor Chen's shed. The door was open. They entered. She had spent time every day in this space, but today it felt different to her although the books and the furniture were exactly the same and the light was shining through the windows as usual.

When both were seated, still no one spoke. Amethyst concentrated on the sounds of their breathing and the clink of three glasses of water as the professor set them down.

The prince spoke first, more slowly and softly than his usual style. 'Amethyst, I have come not just to tell you of my love and my hopes. I want to hear yours. Will you tell me?'

'I have thoughts and deep longing, but no hope for love,' she murmured, 'only for managing without it. I do not wish to talk about it. I cannot do it without crying.'

Professor Chen put a hand on her shoulder. 'Do you want Rio to speak of his hope or go without speaking?'

She thought she could not bear to hear his hopes, but she was not willing to send him away now that he was beside her. 'I will listen.'

The prince sat up straight and looked at Amethyst. 'I have plans, but you may make changes. It is for *our* future.' She thought how handsome he was and how loving. She wanted to do whatever he asked, but it was unlikely that it would work.

After a pause, he continued, 'We must marry, but in secret at first.' He turned to the tutor. 'I am hoping you, Professor, can find us a priest who will perform the ceremony.'

Professor Chen made no reply. He sat without moving and did not indicate what his thoughts were.

'The garden apartment is furnished, ready for us.' His eyes turned to his love. 'And you will be able to choose paintings or other things—make it more your place, more comfortable for you. Once we are married, we will live there in the palace. My father will see that a decision has been made. It might take a while, but he must accept it. One day you will be queen, or if he is so upset that he manages to deny you the title, you will be the royal consort. In any case, our children will be princes and princesses, and one of your children will someday rule Riparia.'

Amethyst sat like a statue. Surely this was a fairy tale.

Professor Chen spoke, 'I have heard that your grandfather brought the lady Florence, who is now queen, unannounced to Riparia and presented her to your father as his bride a week before the marriage.'

Rio sprang to his feet. He towered over them. 'My father would never do that.' There was complete stillness; the prince collapsed back on to his seat. 'Well, yes, my grandfather . . . it was different then.' He put a hand to Amethyst's shoulder. 'My father told me it was hard for him.' He put his hands on hers. 'I could not do that. My father knows I would not. My princess . . .' He picked up and kissed both her hands.

Amethyst thought he had not convinced Professor Chen who seemed perplexed— rubbing his forehead and pulling on an ear as he looked at the prince. Rio continued slowly and deliberately, 'When we are married, when you are my wife, what can my father do? I cannot have two wives. I will live only with you, Amethyst, and with our children. Always.'

The only sound was an imprisoned fly batting in vain at a closed window. Amethyst imagined she was a bit like the fly. The three at the table were silent. The fly changed direction and flew out the open door. Was there a way out?

Amethyst spoke, 'I do not know if it is wise. Perhaps I know it is not. To even think about . . .' Her mouth was a straight line and her wide eyes piercing. She looked from the prince to Professor Chen as if for help. 'I cannot turn away. I think I must . . .' She turned back to the prince. 'But I will consider. I will sleep on it.'

She stood up and reached towards the professor, who rose and went with her to the house.

Rio and his tutor sat up for some hours. They did not speak much, but Rio was comforted by the concern and support of the older man.

Amethyst alternately tossed and dozed. By morning, she had concluded that agreeing with Rio's plan was a great risk, an impossible gamble, but on the other hand, despair was certain if she did not try for a future with the prince.

Chapter 3

The next morning, Amethyst and Rio's happiness made everyone smile. Professor Chen did not mention his concerns. He and his sister agreed that Amethyst could stay until all was settled. The house by the river seemed an ideal spot for the wedding to take place.

Rio returned to the palace. A few days later, when Amethyst went back to the house after helping the professor, she found her hostess, dressed in one of her colourful loose gowns, stretched out on a garden lounge.

She called, 'Come here, child. I hear you are getting married.'

'Yes, my lady.' Amethyst went to her.

'Algernon told me your name. Amethyst, a lovely name. I have something for you.' She pulled a tiny silk pouch from a pocket and held it out. She was actually smiling, and Amethyst realised she did resemble her brother.

'Open it.'

Amethyst did. A single rough-hewn stone fell on to her palm—a purple amethyst. She crouched beside the woman. 'Amethyst, my stone. I've never had a piece before. Oh, thank you, thank you.'

'You are welcome.' The woman's smile faded, and she started to close her eyes, then opened them suddenly. 'What will you wear?'

'I have a nice skirt with a white blouse.'

'I used to wear beautiful clothes.' Remembering, she smiled again. 'No longer need them. Go with Lou. She'll remake whatever you want—a whizz with the sewing machine.' Her eyes closed completely.

Amethyst walked slowly into the house. She felt like dancing with the precious stone, but she went slowly, wondering about this woman in whose home she was living.

Lou took her to a closet so wide it needed three doors. There in front of her were dresses, many of them full length and of every colour. 'We can do anything you want,' Lou said. 'Just pick the material you like, and I'll make it up.'

After about an hour of looking, draping material over her shoulders, and studying patterns, they settled on a white silk blouse with intricate embroidery on the collar and cuffs of the long sleeves. It needed only the tiniest adjustment to fit perfectly. With that, she'd wear a simple long skirt. Lou would sew it, cutting the material from a formal gown which matched her amethyst stone.

Later in the day, she showed the stone to the tutor. He regarded it in silence with his heavy-thinking face. Amethyst was afraid he was upset with his sister for giving it away.

'Was it too much for your sister to give me?'

'No, Amethyst, not at all. I was just thinking—if you wouldn't mind—that I could . . .' He paused and looked at her.

'What, Professor? What is it?'

'Would you trust me with it? I . . . I'd like to show it to someone.' He seemed about to say more, but stopped.

'Professor, I would trust you with anything. I don't really understand . . .'

'I'll not explain, but I would need to borrow it for a time. May I? It won't cost either of us anything.'

She put it carefully back in the silk pouch and handed it to him. 'It will be safe with you.'

'Thank you, Amethyst. It may take a while, but it will be returned.'

* * *

The next morning, Professor Chen left on the early ferry. Amethyst thought he had perhaps gone to Aviol to the street of jewellers to show it to one of them. However, he headed for the palace and found Prince Rio in the newly refurbished apartment.

'Professor, welcome. Have you come for a lesson?' Rio's sudden smile vanished. 'Is something the matter?'

'No, no—just something to show you. Let's sit.'

The professor opened the silk pouch and held out the stone.

'An amethyst! Where did you get it? Are you suggesting I buy it for my wife-to-be?'

'Not possible, it's already hers—a gift from my sister. I had an idea you might like to get a jeweller to design a setting for it to hang from a chain. I asked to borrow it but didn't tell her why. I did say it wouldn't cost her or me.'

The prince laughed. 'Just me. Professor, I'm grateful, a great idea—something graceful, unique. I bet Julio can do it.'

The two of them went into the city centre. Professor Chen made contact with an elderly priest who had been one of his teachers. Rio went to consult Julio.

The professor discovered Father Antonio down at the docks, helping to unload cargo. The priest greeted him warmly. 'Certainly I remember you, Professor. You were a young troublemaker—not easily forgotten.'

'I hope I was not too much of a problem.'

'No, indeed, your sort of troublemakers are the change agents of our world, needing encouragement and, at times, a bit of calming down.'

'I fear I may be continuing to make trouble, but I hope it's in a good cause and that you'll aid and abet me,' Professor Chen replied.

The priest's eyes twinkled. He was short but far from slim, a chubby elf of a man with a semicircle of white beard, white hair that had not been trimmed recently, and the tanned, wrinkled skin of an outdoor worker. 'Partners in crime, is it? I expect I'm your man.'

So the day of the wedding was set. It was to be a secret until it was accomplished, but the prince would bring a couple of guests. Amethyst wanted to tell her mother and have her present on the day, but she had not spoken to her since leaving the palace. Besides, her mother might have told the king and queen. Amethyst was not clear where her mother's final loyalty lay.

As Amethyst and Rio had agreed not to meet until the wedding, she was surprised but delighted one morning to find him at the foot of the stairs when she went down. They hugged happily, but she was curious about the lopsided grin on his face. 'Ri, what is it?'

He tried to look serious, but his teasing gleam won out. 'I've something to give you that's already yours, something brand new and immensely old.'

'Oh, Ri, show me, show me. What is it?'

He led her outside and sat her down on a bench. Then he handed her an oblong velvet box. Amethyst held it. She stroked the purple velvet. 'Oh, Ri.'

'Aren't you going to open it?'

She looked down at the box and slowly lifted the top. Inside was a silver chain attached to a shining swirl of silver—almost like a breaking wave—which flowed around and held a rough-cut amethyst stone. She didn't understand. It looked so like her stone, but . . . 'What? How? Is it my stone?'

'Yes, my princess. It's your stone, just set so you can wear it. Is it all right?'

'More than that. It's splendid, miraculous. Ri, how did—It's more beautiful than before.'

He fastened it round her neck. When they went to show the tutor, he took them to his sister as well. It was a day of joy.

* * *

On the morning of her wedding, she looked out from her window; the river sparkled in the sun. A sea eagle landed in the large tree by the shed. She watched delighted. Sea eagles brought good luck, and this one turned towards her as if the luck was particularly for her.

After breakfast, where she barely managed a piece of toast and a cup of tea, Lou came to help her dress. Both Lou and Jerry were coming to the ceremony. They and the professor were her family.

Professor Chen escorted her. He was, as usual, in loose trousers and kimono-style jacket, but she had never seen the beautifully embroidered one he was wearing for this special day. 'Oh, Professor, what a gorgeous jacket.'

'And you are looking more beautiful than ever, Amethyst.'

'But nervous, Professor, I'm so glad you're with me. You've done so much. It's all due to you.'

'I have a suspicion it's more due to you, my dear. But it's been my privilege to help.'

She walked out the door on his arm. There in the garden was the prince with little Father Antonio. Jerry and Lou stood waiting with their characteristic smiles, and her hostess too was smiling, resting on a garden lounge. The bride gasped with delight when she saw that her mother was there, standing between two strangers.

Sylvia looked a bit confused, perhaps upset, but she was there.

Afterwards, Amethyst could not recall the ceremony exactly or even the meal that followed. It was all a blur—beautiful but indistinct as if it wasn't quite real. She held on to Rio. He introduced her to his two guests, his cousin Lila and a friend, both about his age; they seemed genuinely delighted to meet her. Sylvia gave her a hug and a kiss and was removed by the professor before she could make a negative remark.

Amethyst was now married to Prince Rio of Riparia. The two of them rode in an unmarked coach drawn by two chestnut horses to the palace precinct. They entered the apartment. They were home.

But it took many weeks before it felt like home to the former housemaid.

* * *

Of course, the king and queen were aware that their son was sharing his apartment with a woman—a person whom they knew. Quite possibly, after a short while, they heard that there had been a marriage ceremony.

'You and your pushing me to get that girl to study with Rio,' the king fumed. 'If you'd listened to me, we'd have stopped this thing before it started.'

'It will pass,' she assured him. 'Royals often have mistresses. People get married and unmarried. Don't aggravate the situation.'

Amethyst was sorry the royal parents kept their distance, but more importantly, what was her role to be? Rio wouldn't let her use her housekeeping skills. 'There are maids for that. You're a princess now.'

'But I'm not, Rio. You don't take me with you to functions. I won't be sitting in the royal coach with you as you ride through the streets. I don't even feel able to go up into the royal corridor or the library. Even when I go into the garden—and I love it—I'm always scared that I'll might meet your parents.'

'They'll come round. You'll see. They're not making any fuss. One day they're going to love you.'

'How can they if they never meet me?' she moaned. 'And I'd like to look after the apartment. It would be something to do when you're away being royal.' But he wouldn't hear of it.

However, he was not unsympathetic. He tried hard to make her happy.

Sometimes they took a break from the palace. Rio and Amethyst would spend a few days in a picturesque cottage near the river, in a farming area, or among great towering trees. She would cook for him and act as a wife who was also a homemaker and a housekeeper. Both thrived on these short interludes.

When they had been married about two months, a knock on the door heralded four workmen carrying the doll's house from the royal corridor. They set it up in the apartment's wide hallway under a huge glass dome, which Rio lifted off.

'It's yours,' he told her. 'You're the housekeeper. Rearrange, dust, polish, move things around. Have fun. Do whatever you want.'

At first she was appalled. 'Rio, it's a precious gem from the royal collection! What will your parents say?'

He took her hand and kissed her on the end of her nose. 'You don't yet understand what a spoiled child you've married. I'm the one and only heir. If I want the doll's house in my flat, how can they object?'

Gradually, it became one of her favourite ways to enjoy herself when he wasn't with her.

There were many good times. Sylvia visited; Rio had convinced her that he and Amethyst belonged together. Professor Chen dropped in frequently. Various cousins and friends of Rio's came for evenings of games and conversation. However, Amethyst often felt as if she couldn't join in their chatting and laughter.

Rio didn't understand. 'Amethyst, you're better educated than any of them—and smarter.'

'Not smart enough to know about the things in their lives.'

Gradually, with Lila's help, Amethyst learned the language of small talk and also discovered the interests of her new acquaintances. She began to enjoy their company. Rio felt all was going well and would get even better when his parents came to accept his decision.

On his return from a few days of royal tour with his father, Rio grinned at how comfortable his wife looked resting on the couch with a book—'like a well-groomed pussy cat curled up in its nest.'

'Oh Ri, how funny you are, but how knowing. Perhaps it is a nest. If I'm a pussy cat, you're a Tom, and we're going to have a kitten.'

Rio was thrilled. 'Now, even my father will accept you, and my mother will be so excited to have a grandchild. But not as excited as I am to be a father.'

Amethyst put her hand on his arm. She had stopped smiling and stared hard at him. 'You must get them to come and meet me.'

'I will.'

'When?' He did not answer at first, and she continued, 'We need to get acquainted.'

'Yes, yes. I'll find a good time.'

But the baby arrived before the 'good time'. Although for Rio and Amethyst the birth of their daughter brought great joy, not everyone could join them in rejoicing. For some, it was, at best, a problem.

Rio would never lose the picture from his memory of Amethyst propped up in bed—exhausted but smiling a bigger smile than he imagined she would have if she were crowned queen of Riparia. In her arms, she held their daughter wrapped in a pink blanket.

'Meet your daughter,' she said. 'See, she has your turned-up nose. What shall we call her?'

'Dawn,' he answered. 'She brings the dawn of a new and more wonderful day for all three of us.'

'Oh, Rio, I am so happy and so tired.'

In later years, this scene repeated over and over in his mind.

For two weeks, there was nothing to disturb the peace in the apartment. Sylvia found a friend from Amethyst's childhood to help with the baby. Nina was the daughter of one of the footmen. She now lived outside the palace but was delighted to get the job. Rio spent lots of time at home and spoke of little else except his new daughter when he was elsewhere.

He had been wanting his parents to meet their grandchild and hoped that they might come to visit. At the end of the second week, he decided it required a personal invitation. He went to their section of the palace and found his mother.

She did not give him much of a welcome. 'Why have you been staying away, Rio? You know that your father and I wish to see you often.'

'I've been hoping you would both come to visit your beautiful grandchild.'

She glowered at him. 'We cannot visit you in your present situation, and we do not have a grandchild.'

The prince found he could not speak. He stood staring at his mother. When he found his voice, his thoughts were jumbled.

'But—what? Mother, what . . . do you mean?

She spoke slowly but forcefully, 'Do not pretend with me.'

'Pretend?' He tried to grasp some idea that would make sense of her words.

She stood like an immoveable rock in front of him. A message of terror assaulted him, but he did not know exactly what it was.

At that moment, the door opened, and the king appeared. 'Francesca, Rio, what's going on?'

The queen relaxed. 'Your son', she said, 'needs some help.'

'Help?'

'He appears or pretends to be unaware of facts relating to the heir to the throne of Riparia.'

'Such as?' The king was unclear as to her meaning.

'Tell him what our laws say about the marriage of the heir.' She looked at her son and then spoke again to the king, 'Tell him the rest of it as well. It's time you did.'

Rio felt his legs weakening. He looked at his father.

The king pointed to a chair. 'Sit down, Rio.'

Both men sat, and the queen left the room.

The king spoke, 'What is it you wish to know, my son?'

'Father, I came to invite you and Mother to visit us in our apartment and meet your granddaughter.'

'Oh.' Now the king understood.

'You will love her.'

'Rio, I see what your mother means.' He took a deep breath. 'You have been living with a woman in the palace precincts.'

'We are married, Father, and she is not just "a woman". She is Amethyst, my wife.'

'Yes, yes. But the facts your mother referred to, I believe, have to do with the law that the heir to the throne cannot marry without the permission of the council—advised by the king, of course.'

The prince gaped at his father. Eventually, he managed shakily, 'You . . . you can advise them, Father.'

'I can and I have. Indeed, your mother wished me to tell you about that.' He paused and shifted in his chair as if he was uncomfortable. 'It is time you knew—as your mother said.'

The prince felt frightened.

The king continued, now eager to tell it all quickly. 'In ten days' time, a princess will arrive in Aviol as your wife-to-be. The royal marriage ceremony will take place two weeks later.'

Rio stood up. 'Marriage! I am already married. What do you mean, Father?'

'Just what I have said. As for your marriage, you can renounce it.'

Rio felt that the floor was slipping from under him. He longed to shout 'Never.' but no sound came.

He sat down and held his head in his hands while his father watched.

After a few moments, Rio raised his head and said softly, 'I will never renounce something which has brought me such joy. I am married, and we have a child, Father.'

'Well, that's as may be. I will declare your marriage invalid and that—'

The prince rose from his chair and walked out.

The prince had left the flat that morning with his wide smile and a gentle kiss. He returned with clenched fists. He went in, shut the door, and stood staring with a face of stone at the apartment.

'Rio, what is it?' Amethyst went to him and touched his shoulder. He grabbed her in his arms. She felt a trembling. Was it in him? It felt more like an earthquake; even the floor beneath their feet seemed to shake.

They clung to each other, his head pressing down on hers. Eventually, he spoke, 'We are ruined.' He led her to the couch. He looked straight into her eyes; holding her hands, he told her what his father had said.

'I do not know what to do. I cannot turn my back on my country, but I cannot give you up. You are my life and my love.'

The next day, the prince was summoned to the council chamber. When he again refused to sign a paper declaring his marriage invalid, the king signed it and stamped it with the royal seal. The king explained to the council that the princess who would be arriving in Aviol was not from any of the known royal families. Her father was 'king' of a tiny island and was intent on marrying his three daughters to royalty. He was willing to pay handsomely for the privilege.

He went on to detail plans for the formal ceremony and banquet. 'You will be pleased to know', he said, turning towards his son, 'that we are preparing for you and your bride the palace apartment where your mother and I lived when we were first married.'

Rio did not reply. He stood there silently until his father said, 'You may go. I will send for you again when I need to give you further information.'

The prince returned to Amethyst and found Professor Chen there with her. When Amethyst heard that the king had cancelled their marriage, she was distraught. 'How? How can he? Two years, two whole years we have been married. Rio, we have a child. How? What . . . what shall I do?'

The prince put his hands on her shoulders and squeezed them. He looked steadily into her eyes. 'Amethyst, we are married. Not because a legal paper says so. That's just a piece of dust on a shiny surface. Our hearts are married. Our bodies are married. Our minds are married. We will stay married until we die.'

'But . . . but you will marry someone else. You will live—Oh, Rio, I cannot . . . I do not know . . .' Amethyst sobbed uncontrollably. She felt as though the palace was falling down.

He held her and tried to make his message clear. 'But I will not live with her. She will have to live in whatever place my father gives her, alone. I will live here with you, Amethyst, and our child. You will be my only wife—the only one—no matter what ceremonies and rituals my father drags me through. He cannot make me live with her. He cannot make me sleep with her.'

Professor Chen wondered. 'If he can cancel your marriage—legally—to Amethyst and force you to stand up and make promises to another woman in front of all the powerful people in the land, I'm not sure it's all going to work out as you wish.'

'Maybe you're right, Professor. Perhaps there's a better way. I just haven't had time . . .'

They sat in silence, thinking. Problems and difficulties blotted out possible solutions. Rio was the only one to come up with any ideas. 'I'll meet her and explain that I'm already married—and have a child—so I can't marry her. Then she won't want to marry me. She'll refuse to have anything to do with me and return to wherever she came from.'

'That's certainly a better plan—as long as she goes along with it,' the professor responded.

Amethyst spoke, 'Oh Rio, it's all so awful. For you, for me—I don't think I can . . .' She began to cry again. 'Oh, poor Dawn.' She covered her face with her hands. Then suddenly, she looked up. 'And the princess. What about her? Imagine travelling to a country you've never seen to marry a prince and finding, when you get there, you're not wanted. It's impossible. How can it be happening?'

Chapter 4

As the days passed, it all seemed to be happening according to the king's plan. Rio's idea sank out of sight as soon as it was tried. The Princess Sorra certainly did not wish to be married to anyone. She had begged her father to let her enter the convent. But she refused to return to the tiny island where her father called himself king. She was terrified of his reaction. 'I will be punished—beaten, imprisoned, starved. I will kill myself before I go back.'

The first conversation they had managed to have without others present had made the situation clear. But all was not lost. Rio gave Amethyst a long kiss when he returned. 'She doesn't want marriage to me or anyone. It will work.'

Amethyst wasn't convinced. It was constantly in her mind, and she longed for someone who could advise her. Rio's days were full of luncheons, dinners, and other activities arranged by the king. The prince left early every morning and slipped carefully back under the covers when he returned long after she'd gone to bed. Professor Chen spent time with her and let her talk it through over and over, but 'You'll know what's best' was all the advice he would give.

Her mother was even less help. 'Oh, I knew I should never have let you study with the prince. See what's come of your going out of your proper sphere.'

Amethyst often spoke of her concerns to Nina. 'He'll have even more times away. He and his princess will have to show themselves together to the people. They will have to entertain, to make a good show. He cannot spend time here. In fact, I expect the king will take over this apartment. Oh, Nina, I cannot stay here, but how can I survive without him?'

Nina thought she didn't have a choice. 'Where could you and baby Dawn go? How would you live?'

She certainly didn't know the answer to that question, but how could she stay?

As the wedding day drew nearer, Nina seemed more like a flitting butterfly than a helper. She reported excitedly on the preparations in the kitchen and in the sumptuous apartment in which the heir and his new wife were to live. Her eyes sparkled when she described the decorations of the public spaces prepared for the wedding itself and the banquet to follow.

Gradually, Amethyst was moving to a clear decision. First, for the country and even for Rio's sake, she must leave; he would be pulled apart if she stayed. Secondly, even for her and the baby, it was best. What standing could Dawn have in the palace?

She must not tell anyone. She must plan every step, but no one must suspect that she would even consider leaving.

She set about it carefully. Rio was too busy to notice. Her mother and Nina would not be a problem. It was just with Professor Chen that she would have to be particularly clever.

He was there again, as usual, the next day. She greeted him with a new spirit. 'Oh, Professor, I'm so glad you're here. I've decided to look at the positives instead of the negatives. Maybe you can enjoy my company more now.'

'It is always a pleasure with you, my dear. When you are worried, I am glad to be a sounding board.'

She spoke again before he could go where she did not want him to go. 'Come and see baby Dawn. She is so clever.' Her daughter smiled on cue, and they took her outside into the garden.

The professor asked, 'Have you made a final decision then, Amethyst?'

'You know nothing's final, Professor. I will just have to let things go for a time and see how it all develops.'

'I'm not sure that sounds like my star pupil, but it's probably best for the moment. I wish I could take you to my sister's again, but as you know, she died. The property would have come to me, but her debts were so great it had to go. I still have some resources. You must let me know if I can be of help.'

'Of course, Professor.'

She felt bad about keeping the truth from him, but there was no other way.

She would only have to keep up the pretence until the wedding. That was the time to go, the one night she was sure Rio could not come home.

On the day of the wedding, Rio came through the door a bit before noon. She'd never seen him so pale—and how old he looked. 'I made an excuse. Are you all right? We've got to pretend . . . a honeymoon. Only two nights . . . back Monday.' He grabbed her and kissed her fiercely.

'I need money,' she said. It sounded false and heartless in her ears.

'Of course.' He pulled out his wallet and handed her two bills, one hundred avars each. She had to stop herself from saying it was too much.

Then she was sobbing in his arms. She felt his tears falling on her head. They clung together without speaking, then went through the door into the baby's room. Dawn slept, unaware of the tumult that swirled around her.

'Amethyst, I love you more than ever. As soon as this folderol's over . . . Monday night at least.' He kissed her hard and fast. She held his arm. 'Ri, oh Ri, I love you whatever happens. Remember. Remember. I will always love you.'

He was gone—to his mother's, where his wedding finery lay ready. He would dress and be married with ceremony to the princess who did not want a husband.

Now she had to make sure no one would look for her too soon. Today was Saturday, and she must keep her mother away—hopefully until Monday. She must get rid of Nina somehow.

She wrote a note to her mother. 'I just want to be by myself with the baby for a couple of days. You'll be busy anyway. So please don't visit until at least Monday. I really would prefer just to be with Dawn for a bit. Nina will manage anything I require.'

Nina's mother had been unwell for some weeks—a helpful state of affairs in the circumstances. Amethyst asked Nina to take the note to Sylvia's apartment. 'After you deliver the note, go check on your own mother. Now's the best time. I won't need help for the next few days—my mother's planning to be here. Don't come back until Monday afternoon or later if you're needed.'

'But, Amethyst, I want to see the wedding and all.'

Oh, dear. 'You can do what you like. Off you go. Be back by Tuesday.'

Nina was delighted. 'Thank you, thank you.' She took the note and danced out the door.

Amethyst felt awful about lying to her mother. But how else could she manage?

She set the duffel bag on the bed. It was just big enough; Dawn could sleep in it if there was nowhere else, and it wasn't too big to carry. She packed two sets of Dawn's clothing, one of her own, a pile of nappies, and a bag of items she might want for the baby. Water would be heavy, but she packed one bottle—also a few nuts and two apples. She pulled an old cloak from the back of the cupboard; it could cover both of them. An old waterproof bag of Rio's, two small toys, and a pacifier were tucked in a corner. She slid the purple box, with the amethyst on its silver chain, under everything.

Dawn had woken up whimpering, but she was getting more insistent. Amethyst felt so drained she wondered if she had any milk to give. She cuddled the baby, changed the nappy, and settled into her favourite chair. There was only time for one more feed after this, and that would be her last time to sit there and Dawn's last feed in the palace.

The afternoon went slowly. Everything was ready, and she found she could not rest while she waited for the appropriate time. At 5 p.m. there was always a line of servants who did not live in the palace leaving by a small back door. Today there were fewer than usual; everyone's minds were on the wedding, and no one paid attention to a woman in a cloak who exited with them. No one noticed that she appeared to be carrying much more than was normal or that she did not bother to check her name off at the door.

As she stepped out of the palace and followed the line towards the street, her first thought was 'I am no longer Amethyst. I am Liana with her baby, Aster'. The next was confusion. She knew little about the more-distant parts of the city. She had no idea where to go. She hoped to find a guest house and pay for a few days' lodging while she got her bearings.

She followed the majority of the others. They turned left outside the palace walls, then right over the bridge, where there was a heavy fog. The number in front of her had dwindled by the time they reached the slum area, which was called Shackville.

This was the poorest part of the city. The others dispersed quickly, and Amethyst moved more slowly in the darkening streets, where the fog had become a drizzle. The track was now rough and uncertain—a step on stone followed by soft ground or gravel, which rolled under her feet. When she stopped and looked ahead, there was no one there.

She had hoped to find cheap accommodation and settle for a few days or a week—she had enough money for that—while she looked for work and found a way to care for Dawn, whom she must remember to call Aster. And she was Liana. She must use these new names.

It was too much. At the moment, she could see no way to manage even this one night.

A faint light came from two windows in a house on her left. It looked larger than she would have expected in the area or had seen in the last half hour. However, it was not an answer to her problem. It was not an inn or a guest house.

The bit of light showed her a small structure on the other side of the street. It looked like three-quarters of an abandoned shed. There was no wall on the side towards the road. Inside was a heap of something which turned out to be an old sofa with odd bits of material, possibly discarded carpets and drapes.

At least it had a roof and something on which to lie down. She fed the baby and then wrapped them both in the cloak. She pulled some of the loose material around and over them. Everything felt damp, and there was a whiff of mildew.

The light in the house went out, and she slept—only waking to feed Dawn. She must remember her name was now Aster. They both drifted off again. After the second feeding, the shapes of buildings, and a couple of scraggly trees were visible.

She lay there, pulling apart all the unworkable options which filled her mind. Had she made a terrible mistake by leaving?

Well, she was here now, and she must not let herself be found.

The door of the house opposite opened, and a stocky woman in a dressing gown came out and stood there staring across the road. When Amethyst—who was trying to think of herself as Liana—saw a frown on the woman's face as she plodded across, it felt as though a huge boulder was rolling towards them. It was the end, and there was nothing she could do.

The woman frowned until she was right beside them. Then she smiled. 'Oh, you have a baby, the darling.' She bent over and looked at the sleeping face as the mother pulled back the edge of the covering. 'Where are you going, dear?' Her voice was soft. One could imagine she cared.

'I don't know,' the newly named Liana looked away. 'I guess we can't stay here.' She stood up, laid the child on the couch, and began to fold the collection of coverings.

'My name's Mia,' the woman said, holding out her hand. 'You'd better come with me and have a bite of breakfast.'

* * *

Liana dreamed that they walked across the road and entered a warm, neatly furnished home. There were carpets or rugs in every room and floor-length drapes in the lounge, the smell of toast, and food to eat. Mia took her to an open door. 'This will be your room. You and the baby can stay here for a couple of days.'

She woke from the dream; it was real. She couldn't stop the tears leaking from her eyes.

The rest of the day seemed like an answer to all Liana's and Aster's needs—at least temporarily. Mia was pleased to have company and doted on the baby from the first moment she saw her. No one else came to the house. Liana wondered if there was any chance they might be able to stay for longer than 'a couple of days'.

After she and Aster were settled for the night, she heard shouting and slamming of doors. The next morning, Mia insisted it was nothing to be concerned about.

Several days later, it was a shock when a solidly built man—grubby, unshaven, and loud—burst into the kitchen, where she and Mia were having a cup of tea. Mia was holding Aster and pretending to converse with her.

He pointed at Liana. 'Devil take you, Mia. What's she still here for?'

Liana's growing comfort was shattered in an instant. Aster began to cry, which triggered another shout.

'Shut that kid up, or I will.'

Liana snatched her precious daughter from Mia's arms and fled to their room.

When Mia joined them there, she hugged Liana. 'I'm so, so sorry, sweeting.' She put an arm around Liana, who was cuddling Aster, rocking and humming to the baby while tears rolled down the mother's face. 'I am so sorry,' Mia said again. 'I should have warned you. He's my brother, Hamud. Built the house and all, but he's rough and mean. He never likes it even if I just give a friend a cup of tea.' She put a hand on Liana's shoulder. 'I love having you here. His bark's worse than his bite, and he's not around much.'

Liana didn't know what to say. Were they safe here? Where could they go?

By dinner time, Mia had talked Liana into joining them for the meal, and Aster was asleep.

Hamud looked less frightening and didn't say much. None of them did. It was a solemn meal. Mia's brother ate huge helpings of everything, while the women moved food around on their plates.

That night, Liana had nightmares.

In the morning, she stayed in her room until Mia came to say her brother had gone to work.

Hamud was a builder. Lots of jobs were at a distance, or else he just preferred drinking beer with or without a companion. He often stayed away for a week at a time.

He had no friends and did not want to know the neighbours. 'Scum. Only reason I built here's cheap land.'

Mia's and Liana's friendship deepened quickly. Liana's housekeeping skills and Mia's love of Aster, along with the delight both women had with each other's company, soon stamped the arrangement 'permanent'. Hamud put up with that decision, only questioning it loudly if Aster bothered him in any way. He began to realise that two women could see to his wishes better than one. He spoke seldom; requests came out gruffly. 'Get my slippers' could sound like orders to a firing squad.

Liana put herself out to be pleasant, a stance which Mia had abandoned years before. Liana cooked his favourite meals, prepared sweets she remembered from the royal kitchen, and usually addressed him as Sir. He never thanked her, thinking only that he was now finally being properly appreciated when his evening drink and his slippers were set ready for him when he arrived home.

Liana did not like Hamud, but he was the key to the security she and her daughter needed. Until Aster turned six, life was generally good for Mia, Liana, and especially for the little girl who had the loving care of two women and went to bed every night with her mother. Liana put her to sleep with stories of princes and princesses and was always there in the morning.

Everything changed when Hamud proposed marriage. Liana—worried about consequences which might flow either from accepting or rejecting his offer—clung to Mia when Hamud had left for the day.

Mia was in no doubt. 'You cannot marry him, Liana. He will squeeze you dry.'

'But if I don't, he'll kick me and Aster out into the street.'

Mia insisted she could override any expulsion order from Hamud. But as they cried together and put scenario after scenario through what felt like a butter churn, it became clear to both of them that Liana's marriage to Hamud was the safest path.

As soon as Hamud had built a new small wing on to the house—complete with its own small kitchen—the wedding took place. One of Hamud's drinking pals and a friend of Mia's from the neighbourhood were the only guests and acted as witnesses. The women had made a special 'bridesmaid's' dress for the six-year-old, and she would have looked charming if she had not been fighting so hard to keep from crying.

To Liana, the best thing about the wedding was that Hamud was too busy with building jobs to take a honeymoon.

The first night after the wedding, Hamud dragged Liana off to their wing before she could even settle Aster in the bed they had both shared for six years. Aster cried herself to sleep.

After an early, silent, and inauspicious breakfast for the newlyweds, Hamud went to work, and Liana discovered that Aster was not with Mia.

Shaking, she rushed to her daughter and found her curled up around her pillow, dampening it with new tears. Liana felt like joining her but gave her a big hug. 'Come on, darling, let's do something special today.' Somehow she had to rescue them from the situation in which they were both drowning.

Aster's strangled 'You didn't even kiss me goodnight' was a blow her mother felt through her whole body.

Mia brought in a tray of tea, juice, and fingers of toast. The three of them hugged and kissed and consulted. They came up with a plan. Liana had to sleep with her husband, but she must insist on time with Aster every night—time for a story—and her mother would sit with her for a short while before she went to sleep.

'Any night you wish, you can come in my bed,' Mia offered, and Aster accepted this as her best choice in an unfriendly world.

The older woman and the six-year-old became close in the following year. Liana was still a big part of their lives during the day, but she was unhappy herself and not the mother or the companion she had been. Hamud was generally annoyed with his wife for some reason, often because her daughter refused to even call him uncle although she called his sister aunt. Aster would obey his commands without comment but avoided him as much as possible. She worked willingly with Mia, learning kitchen skills and how to bargain in the markets. Her mother seemed to have lost the impetus to train her daughter as she had been trained.

However, Liana was able to organise some schooling for Aster. An elderly man, who looked vaguely Asian, moved into an old shack which was unoccupied in the next block. For some reason that neither Mia nor Aster understood, Liana began taking food to him and arranged with him to give her daughter lessons. Hamud did not approve, especially not of food leaving the house, but Liana was claiming some power back in the relationship, and the arrangement continued. His name was Mr Chen.

Aster began going daily to Mr Chen's shack, and she came to enjoy the lessons as much as her tutor delighted in her quick mind and infinite curiosity. She loved his stories when they took a recess from classes. She loved his answers to the many questions she had. Only once had he stumbled in answering, when she asked how her mother had gotten acquainted with him and started bringing him food. He seemed to look round the room for an answer and eventually mumbled—which he had never done before—in a disjointed way about how she must keep track of everyone in the street. Aster was sure that didn't fit her mother's ways.

Within two years, life gave Aster another hard slap. Not only must she share her mother with an unpleasant 'uncle' but also with two little babies—twin sisters—who required most of her mother's time. Often Aunt Mia was also busy with the twins, and sometimes she hung over them, Aster thought, as if they were the first babies—or perhaps the only babies—in the world. On the other hand, she herself began to feel rather fond of them although she did not admit it.

When the twins were about six months old, Mia took on a regular time of minding them so that Liana and Aster could do things together. They went walking or stayed at home and talked together.

'When did we come here?' 'Where from?' 'Who is my father?' These were questions which lived in Aster's head and were asked in different ways, but she never got a satisfying answer.

She was told they had come soon after her birth and from far away. 'When you're twelve, I'll tell you more.'

One day Aster remembered her tutor's response to questions about her mother and asked, 'How did you know Mr Chen?' This spoiled that afternoon's chat as her mother just got flustered, gave no answer, and left the room.

Mr Chen had told Aster many stories about the palace, its inhabitants, and its garden. It was also from her tutor that she heard the fable about seeing the sun rise from the palace. There was a park in front of the main palace gates to the west of the palace. In this park was a small hill at the top of which was a large flat stone. If you stood on the stone as the sun rose, it would seem that the sun rose from the palace, and it was said that anyone who stood there just at that time—especially if it was on their birthday—would have their wish granted.

Aster begged her mother to take her there, and finally, her mother agreed that on her twelfth birthday they would go there together. After the sun rose, Liana said she would give her daughter at least some of the answers she was seeking.

Birthdays came slowly, and Aster wondered if she would ever get to twelve.

However, she did discover one answer earlier. She was reading in her bedroom one day when her mother and Mia returned from shopping. They had taken the twins with them and were chattering away to each other as they brought them into the house. Mia's 'But you came from the palace' was answered by Liana's reply of 'Oh, yes, but that's like a dream now'.

The palace. Aster did not tell her mother what she had heard or question her any further, but her imagination could work overtime on that one, and it did.

Maybe her father was the chief chef or perhaps the head gardener. Maybe he was even now living in the palace, and she could meet him. She made up stories in her head and worked out all sorts of different scenarios.

Shortly before Aster's eleventh birthday, Liana became ill. Hamud got upset by the lack of attention to his needs and left. After he had been absent for two weeks, they received a short note from someone of whom they had never heard. Hamud would no longer be responsible for anything connected with the household.

No one missed Hamud, but they had depended on the money he earned. The house was in such an uproar that Aster ran away to Mr Chen, which turned out to be the best thing she could have done.

He came back with Aster. 'I think I can help, not just me. I have enough for myself but not for a household. But I have, well, connections.'

He went to the market and came back with a basket full of food. 'Not to worry. We will manage. You will see.'

He left the area for a whole day, after which Aster often saw the same stranger going to Mr Chen's house. But he would not answer any of her questions about the visitor.

Mia was getting unsteady on her feet. Aches and pains bothered her. She helped as much as she could. Aster and Mr Chen managed.

As her mother got weaker, Aster spent many hours just sitting beside her, sometimes holding a cool cloth on her forehead or feeding her a nourishing broth. At times she received bits of information about her past. One day her mother actually confirmed that she, Aster, had been born in the palace. Another time she showed her an old photograph.

'Why does it say "the lovely Amethyst"?'

'Oh, that's just an old name someone used to call me.'

On one of the better days, her mother took a beautiful purple box from a drawer by the bed. 'Open it, Aster, and wear it round your neck, especially when I'm gone. Then you must keep it with you always.'

'Don't say that, Mother. You're getting better. On my birthday, you and I will go to the little hill and watch the sun rise from the palace, and we will both wish for you to be well.'

'My darling Aster.' Silently, she clung to her daughter's hand and fell asleep.

Chapter 5

After six sons, a seventh one. The winds foretell
where he shall sit upon the throne, all will be well.

The six princes of the Land of Far, where snow covered the ground for ten months every year, knew the rhyme well. Their great-grandparents had known it. Many of the people in the kingdom had unrealistic expectations of the miracles the seventh son would deliver—such as an easier climate, greater wealth, and longer life for everyone.

Until the seventh son came into his own, they knew they would continue to struggle. Much of their living was underground. Their gardens were in specially constructed greenhouses where flowers as well as vegetables and fruit trees grew. There were even some where chickens could be found. Their maintenance required hours of work by many people. Cows and goats were not numerous but were accommodated below living quarters in such a way as to give extra warmth to the people. Most of the year, moving from one place to another meant skiing or using snow shoes. They knew that everything took twice as long and three times as much effort as was required in most other parts of the world.

The Land of Far was even smaller than Riparia. It lay along Riparia's northern border, separated from it by a cliff so steep and high that it had kept the inhabitants of the two countries from either cooperating or fighting. No one had ever been known to cross it. By way of a long circuitous route through other lands, a person could travel from one to the other, but there was no direct communication between the deep-snow country and its warmer neighbour.

Shortly before Amethyst and Prince Rio were married in Riparia, people of the Land of Far were looking forward to a wonderful future because their beloved Queen Beatrice, five years after the birth of Lance, her sixth son, had been delivered of her seventh baby boy, whom they named Maren. There was great rejoicing.

All the Far princes, as they were called, were tall and slim. Most smiled readily, and all worked as hard as the other inhabitants of the land. There was no real palace for the royal family's residence. They lived in one of the larger dwellings. They were well respected and had a couple of helpers living with them. Most of the time, they worked alongside everyone else when it came to looking after the greenhouses and the animals, shovelling snow, and maintaining the buildings.

Some of the boys had the hair and eyes of their mother, and some resembled King Fargo. All were athletic and of high intelligence. As well as the general work in which they participated, each had a particular interest.

Gareth—seventeen at the time of the baby's birth—was the presumed heir. He preferred a future engrossed in the study of history to becoming king and was eager to pass his right to rule on to the fulfiller of the ancient prophecy. There seemed no way he could do so, and it was almost inconceivable that the boy would ever be in a position to rule. However, Gareth hoped that the prophecy had so taken hold of the people's imagination that they would, when the time came, welcome the reign of the youngest brother rather than following the usual custom of the eldest being king.

He led his brothers in guarding the baby's health and welfare. He set in train a program of super education with the aim of preparing this seventh son to be the finest monarch who had ever reigned. He organised each brother to plan a preliminary introduction to their special interest. Harold specialised in mathematics, Igor in philosophy, and Jarrah in science. Kim was an expert skier and camper, while Lance concentrated on the gardens.

Gareth wanted the baby's education to begin almost before his eyes were properly open.

By the time Maren was three, his day was full of wonderful times with each of his brothers. It was all fun as far as the young prince was aware. He loved spending time with his brothers—every one of them—and had no idea he was being educated. The games and stories were full of history, counting, science, and practical skills in gardening and camping in the snow. He did not know he was learning anything when he accompanied his father on visits to the homes of other snow-bound residents or community gatherings.

By the age of ten, he was solving mathematical equations, exploring ideas of different philosophers, keen to do scientific experiments. A boy five or six years older would have struggled to equal his accomplishments.

He could read and write well; his mother had started him writing and reading as soon as he showed the slightest interest. She was competent in languages of several countries nearby, and he enjoyed speaking them with her. He was acquainted with the history of many parts of the world and had a substantial knowledge of gardening from working with Lance. He skied expertly and enjoyed every chance to hike with his brother Kim. He could build an igloo for overnight sleeping and had a good grounding in first aid.

Soon after Maren's eleventh birthday, their mother died. The queen was mourned by the whole kingdom, but the loss to the royal family was huge. She had been the star around which they had all found their orbit, and it was hard to continue without her. However, they pulled together and supported each other in their grief. Gareth and Harold, the second son, had both married hardy mountain girls from the community. Although no one could take the place of Queen Beatrice, the two royal wives tried to be substitute mothers for at least the youngest prince. Maren did not reject their concern, but they weren't his mother. The time he had spent with Queen Beatrice was now claimed by his father. King Fargo felt comforted by Maren's presence as the boy reminded him of Beatrice with his red-brown curls and blue eyes.

By the next year, the icy kingdom had further worries. First, there was a rumour that a marauding force was gathering to the north-west and prepared to march into the Land of Far. Then there was a startling document delivered to the royal residence. No one knew who had brought it or exactly when it had arrived.

This was what it said:

> To all and sundry in the Land of Far, know this—that we, who are of the line of the true rulers of the realm, are coming to claim our rights. We will move with strength into our kingdom and rectify the wrong which was done to our grandparents and their child.
>
> We will spare the lives of all who do not oppose us except for those of the wicked line which cruelly cut down our forebears. They will be destroyed—one and all.
>
> We will bring prosperity and wealth to all who join with us in this enterprise.

It was signed 'Rightful Rulers of the Land of Far'.

King Fargo was able to explain something of the background to the strange story at which the document seemed to hint.

His grandfather was the youngest of three brothers. The middle brother, who was named Gale, was an angry and violent man. Even as a boy, he had bullied his two brothers, and 'accidents' had happened for which he accepted no responsibility but for which there was no explanation unless Gale had engineered them. He had married a woman from the most distant part of the Land of Far. She was evidently not aware of his reputation. Soon after they had a baby girl, two tragedies occurred. First, the eldest brother died when he and Gale were hiking around snow-covered canyons. Then Gale went into a frenzy and attacked his wife with an axe. Three men, hearing the disturbance, entered the house and tried to subdue him. Both Gale and his wife died in the struggle, and the three men were all injured.

It was considered that Gale had 'bad blood', which could be passed down to his daughter, who was less than a year old. Members of the council at the time moved to execute the child, but the surviving brother, who was now heir to the throne (whether the child survived or not as she was female), insisted that she be allowed to live. So she was taken away by ski out of the mountains and then by horse for a great distance.

She was given to a peasant family as an orphan who had no one to care for her.

On receiving the threatening missive, the council met immediately. It was the ruling body of the country and was composed of the king, his sons who were over sixteen (Lance, the youngest, except for Maren, having just joined), and ten extra councillors, three of whom were the head of the army, a legal expert, and a councillor to whom the people brought their wishes, fears, and complaints.

The army chief moved that Prince Maren, the seventh son, be spirited away quickly to another country where he could live incognito for as long as necessary. He felt that in the worst case, if the royal family were all killed, this one, who was—according to the prophecy—destined to rule, must be saved in order to return to lead the country of his birth.

'Perhaps the king of Riparia would keep him safe in his palace,' suggested the king.

'One of us must go with him.' Gareth said. All in the family were shocked at the thought of sending Maren, their little brother, off alone to a strange country where they would have no knowledge of his welfare.

But the councillor pointed out that the safest option was for him to disappear into a country where no one knew of his background and he seemed just an average inhabitant.

Lance, speaking for the first time in a council meeting, proposed that they invite Maren to join them in the discussion. Kim concurred, 'Good plan. He'll be better able to follow our lead if he's aware of our reasons.'

So Maren was summoned. He was a bit awed by the solemnity of the entire council in session, although he knew all of them well. He turned a bit pale when he discovered the subject of the meeting.

Different ideas were put forward, but the consensus was that he should go to Riparia. He was proficient in the language; it was a well run and peaceful country. It bordered the Land of Far, although it was considered impossible to go directly from one country to the other by way of the extremely high and totally sheer cliff. However, they did not dare to take him round by the usual and longer route as they were not sure where members of what they referred to as the Gale Faction might be lurking; it might not be a safe journey.

So Kim, the expert in hiking and climbing, was to work out a way of lowering Maren into Riparia. Some of the group thought that Kim could return from his trip with Maren and declare him missing—lost or dead. But that was ruled out as possibly leading to more complications, such as searching for the body.

It was decided that only those in the council should know of their plans.

Kim studied the situation and spent almost a week making preparations. He decided that he would need extra help lowering his brother. So Kim, Lance, and Maren set out together. They usually enjoyed their expeditions, but this day they looked solemn as they skied away from their home. In late afternoon, they set up camp. The next afternoon, they reached the border.

'There it is.' Kim pointed down to the green land.

'Is that a real house?' Lance wondered. 'Wow, it looks like a toy.'

Maren was charmed by the lack of snow. 'I know they hardly ever have any, but doesn't it look amazing?'

They anchored the immensely long rope to a sturdy tree. Then the three brothers stood staring at one another. They didn't speak—they had said all that could be said. The two older boys grasped their brother's hand and looked into his eyes. Then the three of them threw their arms around each other and held on tightly. They were all full of the same hope: that the troubles would pass quickly so that they could be together again.

Eventually, Kim pulled back and picked up the elaborate leather harness he had constructed over the last week. He and Lance made sure every buckle and connection was secure as they strapped it on to Maren and looped him on to the rope. They began the descent. It was a long, slow process. Kim had never before done such a manoeuvre over such a long distance. Eventually, Maren's feet touched earth. He took off the harness. Waves were exchanged; Kim and Lance began the long job of pulling it all back up.

Maren looked around him. How inappropriate to be wearing these heavy boots. Well, he'd just have to clump about in them till he found something better. It was late afternoon. His first job was to find a place for the night, and he must remember to speak Riparian. A gravel road led him near the house they'd seen from the top of the cliff. It was actually quite large. He walked up the path; the bushes beside it were carefully clipped and the path was neatly edged. A dog barked inside. Maren knocked on the door. It opened a crack.

'What'ye want?' A scrawny man with an angry face appeared; Maren could see the dog straining and slavering beside him.

'I'm looking for a place for the night.'

'Not here, yer not. Get off'r I'll set dog on ye.'

Maren turned with a quick sorry and went back to the road.

It wasn't all that cold. He could sleep out if he had to.

There was another house further along on the opposite side. It had an old sign at the broken gate. He could barely read the words 'Cliff Base'. The bushes needed pruning, and there was a general untidiness as though no one had enough time or strength to finish things properly. One of the steps to the veranda felt a bit wobbly. Maybe they'd give him a job. He stepped up to the door and knocked.

He could hear someone moving. An older man with a face that spoke of gentleness opened the door wide. 'Hello, son, what's te do?'

'I'm looking for a place for the night. I can do some jobs for a spot to lie down.'

'Come on in.' Then he called to someone at the back of the house, 'Jenny, m'love, there's a boy here needs a bed.'

A woman about the same age as the man came up the hall. She had a bent beak of a nose and a chin that stuck out almost as far. But it was her smile that he noticed and how tired they both looked. Maren wanted to sit them both down and look after them.

'Come in. Come in. Have ye eaten? We've bread and soup.' The words tumbled out, and the smile just kept growing.

Maren was overcome by the welcome. He felt out of place in his heavy clothing and boots. 'Thanks so much. I'll just take these off before I come in.'

'Never ye mind. Come in and sit down first.'

They ushered him in almost as if they knew he was royalty; he realised they would have treated any beggar the same.

Jennifer and Jake Tremain were an elderly couple who had lived all their lives at the foot of the cliff but had no idea that anyone could ever descend from the clouds above. They had lost their only son several years before and struggled to keep themselves and survive on their small holding. Jake was a mechanic who did jobs of all kinds. Jenny was a midwife and a shoulder to cry on for many in the surrounding community. Her cakes and soups were part of every gathering.

Maren had knocked on the right door. A room to himself, food, and even suitable clothes were instantly his. They had not given away all of their son's clothes, and what remained fit Maren well enough.

They were not inquisitive. When he said he had come from a long distance, they did not press for further information. He was a boy—almost a young man—who had needs they could meet, and they took him in as their own. When he found it hard to give them his last name, they suggested it would save trouble if he was their nephew, the son of Jake's brother. So he became Maren Tremain, and there were no questions. Jake had a brother who lived at the other end of the country; he had never visited and, as far as they knew, did not have a son.

Maren was eager to be of use. He had the yard looking spick and span in a few days. He had a little Riparian money, with which he purchased some bulbs and a few small pots of pansies and violas. Jenny was thrilled.

'Oh, 'tis beautiful, the colours,' she exclaimed. 'Straight from heav'n.'

He went out working with Jake and heard him tell his wife, 'He's more help'n any two of 'em.'

The Tremains were concerned that Maren should attend school. They asked Katy, the local schoolteacher, to come by. Her first question was 'How old are you, Maren?'

'Nearly thirteen, Miss.'

'Had much schooling?' Katy asked.

'Quite a lot,' he admitted.

When she did a bit of testing, she agreed with that. 'He's way ahead of anyone at the school. Not sure I can teach him much,' she told Jenny.

But Jenny had an idea. 'May be a help. So many in class. Could be he'd help out—teacher's aide or what?'

So Katy gave Maren a job. He was paid a small wage, which he delivered directly to Jenny.

'Oh, no, Maren. That's y'rs, and they don't pay much.'

'More than that's yours. You feed, clothe, and look after me. Couldn't sleep if I kept it.'

It helped the household to have another contributor. They had meat more often; it was good for all three of them.

One of the parents at the school had a large plant nursery. Maren asked if he could join them at the weekends and learn. 'If y'er not in the way so,' he was told.

On the next Saturday morning, he turned up at seven to find work well under way. The boss sent him with a long-time worker Nate to move plants around. Nate was about fifty and had been around plants all his life. He could tell Maren the name of every plant they moved.

'They're m'friends,' he told the boy. 'Don't fergit yer friends' names, do ye?'

Nate enjoyed the company, especially of someone with such eager curiosity. Every Saturday Maren gained a bit more knowledge about Riparian gardens. Both enjoyed the time together.

After more than three years, it was Nate who decided Maren must be sent to the Horticulture College on the outskirts of Aviol. 'He's bright 'n' good at his job. Make a proper gard'ner of 'im.'

He'd never been paid anything for the work he'd done with Nate. Now the boss made up for that and paid the fees for the training. The schoolteacher, Katy, had parents who lived near the college and gave him a thin mattress and a piece of floor to sleep on during the week. All the weekends he spent with Jake and Jenny.

They were just a bit frailer than they had been when he first came to live with them. Each weekend, he took care of any jobs needing doing. To keep up what he considered his share of the finances, he took a job at the college and did odd jobs in the maintenance line when they came up.

How strangely his life had changed. He wondered what was going on in the Land of Far. There was no definite information, and no one came to take him back. Riparia was not often visited by travellers from the mountain kingdom, but even these days, there were occasional tales of a small skirmish with conflicting reports of the outcomes. He had heard whispers about surviving members of the Gale Faction moving into various countries, looking for a royal child who was said to have been spirited away at the time of the main attack. He wished he had a way to learn news of his family. He felt he was still under orders to stay until summoned, and in addition, he now had responsibilities in Riparia. He consoled himself with the thought that he could only live one life at a time.

After two and a half years at the college, he went 'home' to the Tremains one weekend and found that Jake and Jenny were in need of more care. He planned to stop his course and concentrate on the two, who'd helped him so much.

Jenny was adamant. 'No, no, Maren. Graduate with t' diploma ye must. Jobs is not easy.'

She cried when he said, 'You're more important to me.'

However, Jenny and Jake were part of a small but close community. So many people were willing to give up half a day or more that Maren was able to continue his study and the Tremains were well looked after.

Only Jenny was able to see him receive his diploma. She reported in such detail to Jake he almost felt he'd been present. Maren realised how much it had meant to them that he finished when he saw how happy and proud they both were.

Employers wanting gardeners always checked out new diploma-holders. Maren, as top of the class, was offered four jobs—one by Nate's boss, close to the Tremains, and three in Aviol. For Maren, there was only one option.

But Katy was there when the letters of offer were opened. She picked up his discarded pile and had a look. She nearly screamed, 'Maren Tremain, didn't you read this?'

'What, Katy? Those are too far away.'

'Too far away, my hat!' She glowered at him. 'This is an offer to work in the royal gardens, some of the most beautiful anywhere—and the best pay.'

Jenny had heard. 'An offer t' work in royal gardens?'

'Yes, indeed,' Katy confirmed, 'and he's throwing the letter away.'

Maren looked annoyed. 'It's my job, my business. Keep out of it, Katy.'

Katy let it go. She had alerted Jenny.

Jenny had a way of helping people to follow the course she thought right for them. 'Maren, do ye want work wi' Nate, or is it te be close te this house?'

'You're wanting me further away?'

'Balmy, ye be. But ye must know me 'n' Jake can't stay here forever. Jus' thought . . .' She sat quietly for a moment and then, 'Never mind me. Is up te ye.'

He crossed the room and stood by her chair. 'Jenny Tremain, what are you trying to say?'

'Nothin' ye be needin' te hear. It's yer life.'

'And who's been mother to me for six years? You're a canny sort of mother with always a thought or two about the whats and wheres for friends and family. Out with it—what is your plan for my life?' Maren was laughing as he spoke. He leaned over and kissed Jenny on the cheek.

She had to smile back at him. 'The money might come in handy.'

'Come on, Jenny. Money's never the main point with you.'

'Nor 'tis, really. But Maren, Jake and I'll hev te leave this house.' She lost her smile at the thought. 'Could end up anywhere . . .' Then she smiled again. 'Might be we move te royal palace!'

'Best place for you, I reckon. You'd be a great queen.' They laughed together. 'But seriously, Jenny, are you really thinking to leave Cliff Base?'

'We kin think it or not, but we be goin' . . . 'n' might be soon er late.'

He sat down beside her while they talked through possibilities.

Jenny was firm in her confidence that what was good for Maren must, of necessity, be full of good fortune for her and Jake. She just had to convince Maren.

He agreed to at least find out if work in the royal gardens would let him comfortably fulfil what he thought of as his prime responsibility. If Jenny and Jake were well cared for and he could visit them frequently, then he would take the job.

The next morning, he approached the grand iron gates of the palace grounds. He was stopped by a tall guard who was marvellously attired. The uniform was light brown; the epaulets, embroidered cuffs, and a wide diagonal sash across his chest were dark green and sky blue. The guard sent him to a back gate where a man in a deep-green worker's uniform, with the royal seal on the shirt pocket, let him in and directed him to a single-storey building which looked like a storage shed. At the near end were windows and an open door. Maren knocked on the doorjamb.

'Come in,' boomed a voice. A man—nearly bald and slightly shorter than Maren—rose from a desk and went towards him. 'Hello,' he said, 'I'm Brad, head gardener. What can I do for you?'

'I've a letter about employment here.'

'Your name?'

'Maren Tremain.'

'Well, Maren, do you want the job? It's yours if you do.'

'I need to ask a few questions.'

'Oh? Don't think we're good enough for you, boy?'

'Not at all. I've got elderly parents . . . just need to be sure I can still help them.'

'Can't bring them here.' Brad's tone of voice made Maren think he was about to lose the job—which was OK. Jenny and Jake were his focus.

'No, sir, but could you tell me what the arrangements are for time off?'

Brad frowned. 'We like staff here who are interested in the work, not just the time off.'

Maren felt disheartened. 'Thanks for your time,' he said. 'I guess I'd better look elsewhere.' He turned to go.

'Hang on. You going to let me answer your questions?'

'If you wish.' Maren stood still.

Brad shifted his weight from one foot to the other. 'Perhaps I've got the wrong end of the stick.' He pulled a nearby chair closer and turned the one at his desk round. 'Have a seat. Let's start again. What do you need to know before you consider joining us?'

Chapter 6

Her mother was dead. Aster felt like a young tree that has been cut from its roots. If Aunt Mia could have managed without her, she might have given up.

Aster was the only one who could race with her twin sisters, Lia and Loa, when they needed to use up their three-year-old energy. Aster was the one who went to the market to bargain for food. Aster was the one who did the kitchen and cleaning jobs that were too difficult for Mia. So she had to keep going.

Although Mia tried, real support for Aster came only from Mr Chen. She went to him within a ball of darkness, and he managed to let in shafts of light when he spoke of her mother's goodness and his respect for Liana.

Sluggishly the days passed. One morning, Aster woke and was able to notice that the sun was shining. Her next thought was that her birthday—her twelfth birthday—was in five days' time.

There was now no mother to give her more information about her past or—what was, perhaps, more upsetting—to take her to the rock from which she could see the sun rise out of the royal palace, the palace where she knew she had been born.

How could she now learn anything about her father? How could she get other questions answered? However, she could go to the rock—and she would. On her birthday, even without her mother, she would stand on that rock as the sun rose and make her wish.

She had no idea how to get there, but Mr Chen would know. A geography lesson. She needed a lesson in the geography of the city.

As soon as Aunt Mia was settled with her mending and her job of watching the twins, Aster ran down the road.

Mr Chen was pleased with any interest in recommencing lessons. He spread out a map of the city, and they bent over it.

'The rock, where's the rock, Mr Chen?'

'Right here—about the middle of the city. But this is where we are.'

'Show me, show me on the map. How would you go if you walked there?'

He took a red pencil and marked their location, the short lane to the market, and the long, slightly wavy road that crossed four sections of the map and ran to the river. 'Across the bridge, then the rock's on your right.' He finished the line and made a cross on the map.

'How long would it take?'

'What? Are you planning to go?'

'I might . . . someday.'

As he showed her the way again, he told stories of happenings along the route and described some of the things to be seen.

Aster listened carefully, hoping she was taking it all in with three ears, not just two. She drew a small map of the journey, trying to make all the distances to the correct scale.

Mr Chen put a hand on her shoulder and stared hard at her. 'Aster, if you ever want to go there, you must tell me. We can go together. A map of the city is not the same as the city. I do not want to lose you.'

'It's late. I must go home.' She escaped out the door.

She made her plans as carefully as someone about to put all their funds into a new business.

How long would it take to walk to the rock? When she went to the market, it took hardly any time to get there. The road to the bridge was more than ten times as long, and then there would be the bridge to cross and the hill to climb. She didn't know how to figure it out, but she was afraid to ask Mr Chen any more questions on the subject. In fact, she made no more requests for geography and tried to take immense interest in anything else.

She decided to plan for three-quarters of an hour. In the market, she found a discarded newspaper, which showed the time for sunrise as 5.13 a.m. She must leave home before 4.30 a.m.

The night before her birthday, after the twins were settled in the bed the three of them shared, she wrote a note.

'Dear Aunt Mia, it is my birthday. I will be away for a couple of hours—it's a birthday present. Don't worry. I will be back soon. I love you. Aster.'

After Mia was in bed, Aster borrowed the clock from the kitchen and, fully dressed with her mother's special chain round her neck, climbed in beside the sleeping twins. She did not set the alarm but spent the night checking the time. At 4.15 a.m., she lifted herself out of the bed, managing to rock it only slightly. She stepped noiselessly across the floor, returned the clock, put the note under the teapot, picked up her sandals, and eased open the front door. She shut it gently and slipped her feet into her sandals. She went through the gate and walked down the lane towards the market.

There was none of the usual bustle at the market, only one light across on the far side and small scuttling which could almost be leaves moving in the breeze but were probably mice or rats.

Feeling in her pocket for the copy of the map, she turned left and tried to hold her head up and her body steady. She attempted to ignore the slight feeling of nausea in her stomach. It was not totally dark; the moon was up there, giving her as much light as it could, and there was an occasional window lit perhaps by a candle. Her eyes adjusted.

Although she wanted to hurry, she had to move slowly over the ruts and chunks of rock which made up the roadway. Her muscles tightened and seemed to slow her even more when she heard noises—a dog barking or something unknown rustling nearby in the rubble.

As the houses became larger, there were more dogs, but the fences were higher and stronger, and none of the dogs actually appeared.

She tried to sing to take her mind off the shifting shadows and the loneliness. No sound came. She tried to remember the interesting facts Professor Chen had told her, but her mind had lost them all. She kept on—one step after another. How much time had passed? Would she be there before the sun rose?

After what felt like hours, she saw two other people coming into the road ahead. She saw that on the bridge over the river, there were more people all going in the same direction—towards the palace. It was getting lighter, but she was almost there.

When she got to the bridge, the surface was smooth, and she was filled with new energy. She began to run. She saw the palace—a dark bulk in the distance. She came to the hill. The light was strengthening. She powered up the hill and barely managed to remain upright when she reached the rock. She was taking deep breaths, and her mind was working on the exact words to use for her wish.

As the beams of the sun began to colour the clouds, she clasped her hands tightly together and wished for the answer to a question she knew was most unlikely to be answered—who was her father?

As the sun rose—seemingly out of the palace—she held her breath. The glorious pink disappeared, and the brilliance spread around her. There in front of her was the palace, not a dark bulk but a building with towers and extensions surrounded by gardens. She was thrilled, and instead of going home as soon as the sun had risen, she found herself hurrying down the hill to the front gate of the palace.

She held tightly to the bars of the magnificent gate and drank in the sight. Had she really been born in such a splendid place? Her face was against the bars, her nose pointing between them. She did not think she could stop looking.

'On your way. No hanging about here.' The voice was rough.

She looked up to see an angry uniformed soldier waving her away. She backed up, almost tumbling over a rock, and moved to her right where she found a spot behind a large stone pillar. The soldier could not see her there, and she continued her study of the fascinating structure.

She was aware of a well-dressed gentleman passing her and approaching the gate. She backed up to watch him and was spotted by the soldier.

'I told you to go. Get off.'

She started to move further away, but the gentleman called to her to wait.

'No,' he said to the soldier, 'any child can look at the palace. Don't stop them.' He turned to Aster and spoke more softly, 'Do you live nearby?'

'No.' She swallowed. She was shaking inside.

But he was trying to reassure her. 'What do you like about the palace?'

'I was born there,' she managed the sentence without faltering.

The gentleman had known the royal family all his life. Twelve years ago, his father had been the chief councillor. He knew of the baby who had been born then and had never been found in spite of all the searches that had been organised. The king had told him there would be no meetings of the council today as it was the anniversary of the baby's birth. The king planned to spend the day in the garden pergola, where he used to sit with the woman he loved, the mother of their baby.

The gentleman looked at Aster. 'Oh, you were born here? How long ago was that?'

'Twelve years.' She gave him a weak smile.

He tried not to let excitement alter his voice. 'Well, so you're twelve years old. When . . . what day—'

'Today,' she answered before he managed to finish the question.

Although he said 'Happy Birthday', his thoughts and words tumbled chaotically. 'Could—how about . . . how would you like to see inside the palace?'

She looked startled. He wanted to hold on to her in case she fled, but that might scare her even more.

However, Aster was not scared. She did not think this could be real. Was she still at home, asleep and dreaming in her bed?

'As it's your birthday, I think you should have a look inside the place where you were born, don't you?' He held out his hand and prayed she wouldn't dart away.

She placed her hand in his, and they walked through the gate, past the stiff and staring soldier. They did not go up the grand staircase leading to the front door but walked to a door at the side of the palace.

'I'm one of the king's councillors. You can call me Uncle Kahlid.'

She would have to remember this dream; Aunt Mia would love it.

'What's your name?'

'Aster.'

That wasn't the baby's name, but . . . 'Where's your mother, Aster?'

'She died.' At that point, the dream seemed to dissolve into something real.

Kahlid organised food for Aster and sat with her in his office, trying to check her story. Her mother had told her she was born in the palace and agreed to bring her to see it on her twelfth birthday. But was this truly the child for whom they had searched so unsuccessfully?

His secretary hunted up an old photo of the woman beloved by the prince and never forgotten—even now that he was king and had a legal wife, a princess from another country. Kahlid sat the photo on the table as they talked.

Aster stared at it. 'That's my mother. She showed me a picture like that, and she gave me this.' She pulled at the chain of tiny links around her neck and held up a pendant. There in front of his eyes was the amethyst set in silver which the prince, who was now king, had given the woman called Amethyst shortly before they were married.

The questioner paused and took a deep breath. 'What was your mother's name?'

'Liana.'

Had she changed both names? Everything fit except for the names. 'Have you ever heard of anyone called Amethyst or Dawn?'

'Not Dawn, but the name on the picture she showed me was Amethyst. My mother said it was just an old name someone had called her long ago.'

So it was, he thought.

Aster felt she was dreaming again when a crisp, new smock with the king's badge on the left lapel covered her old clothes. Kahlid hoped this would get them past the eyes of all who saw them without triggering any interest. The dream-maker, which was her private assessment of the gentleman, took her through grand hallways where there was so much to see that she could not keep her mind on what she was being told.

He had thought perhaps to let Aster go alone to the king with a morning snack. On the tray he carried, he had placed a note with the story he had been uncovering. But Aster was overcome by the grandness of everything around her and her inappropriateness in the setting. Just before they reached the outside door, she wilted.

'I need to go home.' She looked to the left and right as if searching for a way of escape.

The councillor set the tray down and sat in order to have his eyes on the child's level. 'Aster, you are a strong person, or you would not have come this far. The king has been looking for you for twelve years. He will—'

Aster put her fingers gently on the councillor's lips. 'Why? Why would he look for me?'

Should he tell her or let the king do it? Should he have gone to the king first, by himself? He stood up. 'Come, we will go together.' He picked up the tray, opened the door, and led the child into the garden.

The king was alone in the pergola. He greeted his councillor without much interest and did not seem to notice Aster, who stood and considered him gravely.

'Your Majesty, I have brought someone for whom you have been looking for a long time.'

'Oh.' The king looked up and noticed Aster. He gave her a nod. 'Who is this, Kahlid?'

He was handed the note and opened it slowly. His reaction was abrupt. 'Are you sure? Come here, child. Let me look at you.'

He stared at Aster. His look was fierce. He turned to Kahlid. 'She's not my daughter. Look at her, nothing like Amethyst—wrong hair, wrong face. Ought to be ashamed of herself . . .'

He turned back towards the child, but she was running from them—past trees, bushes, and garden beds. She heard Kahlid call her to come back, but she kept going. When she came to the solid high wall surrounding the palace grounds, she turned left; to the right was the main gate with the uniformed soldier. Maybe there was a smaller gate. She heard Kahlid and then others calling and searching.

She fled—in terror now—although she could not have explained her overwhelming fear. She almost missed the gate. The bushes were thick by the wall, and she was in such a hurry. It was a very small gate, filling a space that had been roughly cut out of the wall. It was rusty and broken; the chain and the lock were firm, but the hinges had fallen off. She slipped out, set the gate back in place, and ran down a narrow track away from the palace grounds. The track veered to the right and then left. She had no idea where she was, but she did not think they would find her in a hurry.

She realised she was still wearing the smock of a royal servant. She slipped it off, rolled it up, and held on to it. No point in leaving it as a clue for someone to find.

Aster walked and walked. She began to worry about how Aunt Mia was managing without her. She must find her way home, but she had no idea how.

When she came to a road, it was packed with people, cattle, horses, and carts moving both ways. She decided to go right and trudged along, looking for someone who might give her directions. She started to approach a boy carrying a large bag that looked as though it was full of potatoes, but he moved too quickly and was soon well past her.

She heard a voice behind her. 'Want a ride, me girlie?' An old man on a wagon drawn by a bony horse caught up with her. He gave her a hand up, and she joined him on the seat. The wagon was full of pumpkins, onions, carrots, and other vegetables. There were three chickens in a cage at the back.

'Where be ye goin?' he asked.

'I'm lost. Do you know Shackville?'

He laughed. 'Lost, is it? No. Nearly there, te be sure.'

He was going to the market, her market. She would be home in no time.

When they got there, she thanked the farmer three or four times and rushed away. She barged into the house and startled Mia and the twins, who were in the kitchen. 'Oh, my goodness, Aster. Are you all right?'

Mia pulled a chair out, and Aster sat, panting. 'I'm sorry . . . Aunt Mia . . . I didn't mean . . . to be away so long.'

'There. Your birthday and all.'

The twins chimed in together, 'Happy Birthday, Aster.'

She was home, back with the people who loved her. Maybe she would do better to stay where she belonged and not chase after answers to questions that were, perhaps, better unasked.

By the end of the afternoon, Aster had been to the market and tried to exhaust the twins with energetic games.

'Will you be able to manage if I go to Mr Chen's for a bit?' she asked Mia.

'Off you go and bring him back with you for dinner.' She smiled at Aster. 'It's a special one.'

Mr Chen greeted Aster and wished her a happy birthday. He was surprised that she looked tired and despondent, not her usual self. 'A hard day on your birthday?' he asked.

'Oh, Mr Chen.' She sank down on the couch and covered her face with her hands. Then she looked up at him. 'I have been so silly. I don't know if I can even tell you all that has happened.'

He sat down beside her. 'Can you begin at the beginning?'

'I don't know. It's so awful. The king was so angry he—'

Mr Chen interrupted, 'The king? What do you mean?'

'I went to the palace. A man took me to the king, and he shouted and . . .' Aster paused and looked as though she was about to cry.

Mr Chen was having trouble making sense of what she was saying. He tried to think of some connecting link that might help. 'Aster, did you go to the Wishing Hill?'

'Yes.'

'And you made a wish?'

She nodded.

'Do you want to tell me what it was?'

She spoke in a weak voice. 'I wanted to know who my father was.'

The tutor was hoping that he could soon add two and two together and get a positive number for an answer. 'After you wished, what did you do then?'

She began to tell him about looking at the palace and being taken into it by a 'well-dressed gentleman.'

'Did he give his name?'

'He said he was one of the king's counsellors and that I could call him Uncle Kahlid.'

Oh, yes, Kahlid. Mr Chen nodded his head. He knew Kahlid. 'But surely he didn't just see you looking at the palace and take you inside without a few questions.'

'Well, he didn't ask me my name or where I came from. It was just that he found out it was my birthday and wanted to give me a birthday look because I was born there.'

Mr Chen was quite sure there was more to it than that. Gradually, he got Aster's side of the story. 'Uncle Kahlid thought the king was looking for me, but he wasn't. He wasn't at all. He was very angry with me for coming.'

'The king was angry? Aster, are you sure about this? This isn't one of your made-up stories?'

'Oh, no.' She looked as serious as he had ever seen her. 'He looked at me as though he would like to kill me, and he shouted at Uncle Kahlid that it wasn't true, whatever it was.'

'What happened then?'

'I ran and ran—away from them. I ran behind trees and bushes, faster than I've ever run. I came to a huge wall.' She told him how she followed the wall and found the little gate. 'I almost missed it. There were so many thick bushes around it.'

Mr Chen wondered if he was really hearing all this. Could it have actually happened?

Aster told of finding her way at last to a road and getting a ride to the market.

He was sure Kahlid would not have taken Aster into the palace unless he had picked up a link between this poorly dressed child and the lost daughter of the king. He would not have taken her to the king unless he had been absolutely positive she was his daughter, which Mr Chen knew she was. How had it gone so wrong? She was now traumatised by the meeting which should have brought them both happiness.

It was perhaps even his fault that it had happened this way. He felt some blame as he could have at any time set things in motion to restore the king's daughter to her father. He had kept quiet because Liana, whom he had known as Amethyst, had shown him the value of bringing up the princess away from the past king and queen. But since Rio had become king . . .

He had been pondering and had said nothing for some time.

Aster touched his hand, 'Mr Chen, what is the matter?'

'My dear Aster, I think I have been a bad friend to you.'

She looked aghast. 'You are my best friend, always.'

'I shall try to be,' he promised.

When he told her that the Wishing Hill had once again fulfilled the prophecy and even let her meet the king, who was her father, she refused to believe him. 'No. Oh, no. He is not my father. Maybe Uncle Kahlid is my father.'

'Aster, I assure you that the king is your father, and at this moment, he is more miserable than you have ever been, even when your mother died.'

She was quite sure Mr Chen was mistaken. The king was angry, not miserable—certainly nothing like the way she felt after her mother's death.

Chapter 7

Meanwhile, at the palace, the king was desolate. It hadn't taken much time for him to understand that he had made a huge blunder. Kahlid told him about the pendant and pointed out that the child he had brought into the palace resembled the king—with tawny hair and a turned-up nose—not her mother.

Gardeners and soldiers were kept searching for much longer than was useful, and everyone in the grounds was told to keep their eyes open. Maybe she had not escaped; perhaps she was still in hiding.

The king wanted to go out himself into the streets and hunt for his daughter. However, Queen Soora and Kahlid managed to convince him that could only make the situation worse.

Rumours were already flying far: one about a beggar child who tried to pretend she was the king's daughter and another about the king having a hallucination and thinking he had found her.

Most of Shackville had not yet heard the rumours, which would soon arrive in strength when the members of the palace staff who lived there returned home.

Before Mr Chen and Aster went to dinner, he had not only done his best to repair Aster's view of the king but also sent a message through a boy runner to Kahlid.

The next day, there was a knock on the door of Mia's house. Aster went to answer it and found Uncle Kahlid standing there. Behind him was a man in a servant's uniform, holding a large basket.

'Who is it?' called Aunt Mia. When there was no answer, she hobbled round from the kitchen. Aster was standing in the doorway, with her arms crossed, staring at a person Mia did not know.

Kahlid spoke, 'Excuse me for arriving unexpectedly. I was hoping to see Aster again and to meet you, Madame, although I do not know your name.'

'I am Mia.' She was always hospitable. 'You are welcome. I will get Aster to show you our main room, and we will bring you tea.' She motioned to Aster, who did not appear to see or hear her.

Kahlid was cautious. Maybe it was not wise to enter Aster's home at the moment. 'I do not need to come in. I will just leave this basket. It is for you and the family.' He took it from the servant and set it on a table at the door.

He thought Aster had relaxed a bit, but he looked at Mia as he continued. 'Professor Chen told me how to find this house. I would like to see him. He suggested that Aster could show me the way.'

If Mr Chen wanted her to do anything, Aster was ready. She uncrossed her arms and took a step towards Kahlid. He did not dare offer his hand to her, but he bowed to Mia and turned back to the road. When Aster followed him out, she saw that a horse and a light, open, four-wheeled carriage stood at the door. Wagons were common but not carriages in this part of town. She stared at it and at the two servants who stood beside it.

'Should we go in the chaise?' he asked.

That actually got a tiny smile. 'We're nearly there already.'

'Will you take me?' He held out his hand hopefully. She took it, and they walked together.

The street was rough, and there was litter everywhere. Most of the houses looked quite temporary. Mr Chen's was no exception. Aster was used to rushing right in, but Kahlid restrained her and knocked. When the door opened, the two men faced each other without speaking.

Then Kahlid said, 'So this is where you have been living.'

Mr Chen just motioned them inside. When they were seated, he said, 'Thank you, Aster, for bringing my friend.'

Aster was surprised. 'Is he your friend? When did you meet him?'

'Before your father and mother met. Long ago. He is my friend, and he will be a good friend to you.'

Uncle Kahlid did not look or sound friendly when he asked the next question, which perplexed the listening child greatly. 'How long have you known who Aster is?'

'Since soon after I moved here when the old king felt I was no longer needed.'

'Did you not know that the whole country and beyond was being searched for the mother and the child?'

'I was aware of it, yes. But after talking with Amethyst, or Liana as she was here, I did what seemed best to me.'

Kahlid did not know what to say. He sat in thought. Mr Chen saw that Aster was anxious, so he winked at her. She relaxed; she knew he could fix any situation.

Kahlid had more questions. 'Have you been teaching Aster?'

'Yes. She has been my pupil for some years. I have tried to prepare her in order that she might—if an occasion ever arose—be able to take up a very different life than the one she has been living.'

'Have you been supporting the princess and her family here?'

'No. At first, Mia's brother had a good job as a builder, and they got on well. Later, when they were in need, I did not have funds, but I organised help. I have always kept in touch with what was happening.'

'Did you know what was happening yesterday? Did you send Aster to the palace?'

After that, it seemed that all three of them were talking at once or suddenly sitting in silence. It was a while before the professor understood the full story of how Aster had met Kahlid and then the king.

The conversation continued. The two men had known each other when the tutor was living in the palace precinct. They spoke of their lives since that time and moved on to options possible for rescuing the present situation.

Aster's eyes began to close. She was on a couch and gradually sank back on to the cushions and was nearly asleep when she heard Kahlid say, 'We must return her to the king.'

'No!' She sat up with wide open eyes.

Mr Chen put a hand on her shoulder. 'What is it, Aster? "No" what?'

'I cannot go back to the king. He does not want me. He hates me.'

Mr Chen kept his hand on her shoulder. 'No, Aster. He may hate himself for what you heard him say, but you are the daughter he has been seeking for twelve years. All he wants is to shower you with love. Only now he is afraid that you will never let him do that.'

Kahlid agreed, 'At the moment he cannot think about anything except finding you again. He is not thinking about the kingdom or anyone else in it. He told me that he had a firm idea that his daughter would look almost exactly like her mother. When he was presented with someone who looked quite different—very like himself—he was stunned. He had just been thinking about you and imagining you, but not as you are. We had startled him out of his daydream, and because you did not fit the daydream, his disappointment overflowed.'

Aster and her two companions sat, thinking.

Mr Chen broke the silence. 'Aster, one day you will be an excellent queen, but it may be that the decisions you make this week in regard to your father will be some of the hardest you will ever make—and some of the most important.'

'Mr Chen,' she said, 'I do not understand. What decisions can I make? I am not the king. I am just a twelve-year-old girl. The king makes decisions. You and Uncle Kahlid make decisions.'

'Usually,' Kahlid agreed, 'but this time you are in charge. I have convinced the king that after what happened, even if you are found again—he doesn't yet know you have been—you cannot be forced to join him in the palace. It is up to you whether you stay in Shackville, move into a home better suited to a princess, or join him in the palace.'

'Can I stay in Shackville?' she asked.

Kahlid replied, 'Possibly, but you will be a princess, and word will get out about the king's daughter living in the slums. Life, even here, would be very different and, I think, extremely difficult.'

'Could I still go to the market for Aunt Mia and have lessons with Mr Chen?'

She was told that lessons with Mr Chen were not in question, but that going to the market would have to be done by others who would come to help.

'But they will not get the best prices. I know the sellers, and they are my friends. They will get charged more.'

Kahlid smiled to himself. This child might reform the royal budget. But he should make it plain that whatever she decided, things would change. 'For you, it may be sad not to be Aster, not to live as you have been living. You are the Princess Dawn. Many things will change. Most of the people you have known will no longer feel they can be your friends. You will not be able to go and come freely, especially here in Shackville.' 'However'—he had a bright thought—'before they find out, would you take me to the market? We can buy some fish or chicken for your family.'

This was returning to what she knew. The idea delighted her. 'We will go to Mr Vino. He has both, and he is always glad to see me.' She stood up.

'I think it must be time to go.' Mr Chen smiled.

Mr Chen went to Mia's house to explain the situation to her while Kahlid and Aster walked together to the market. He marvelled at the competence Aster showed.

The market was crowded and noisy. Hawkers boasted of their wares, shoppers argued over prices, people called to one another, and children were everywhere—running, squealing, shouting, and sometimes quietly thieving a piece of fruit.

Aster moved through the crowds easily, pulling her companion along. Mr Vino greeted her with a huge smile. 'I have saved for you a beeg fish.' He saw Kahlid. 'Thees man is friend?'

'Yes,' she said, 'he's helping me. I wanted him to meet you. A big fish is just what we want, Mr Vino. How much?'

'For you today and friend, a geeft from Vino.' He reached into the ice and held up a whole fish longer than her forearm. He wrapped it and handed it to Kahlid. Aster said a loud, 'Thank you, Mr Vino.'

He smiled. 'Eenjoy.' And he turned to the next customer.

'Uncle Kahlid,' she said when they were out of the market chaos, 'we should have paid him something. If I am to be a princess, I cannot take gifts from people who are not rich.'

'You think like your father,' he answered, 'but just for now we are not telling everyone that you are the princess. He thought you were poorer than he was, and he is fond of you. It pleased him to give you the fish.'

'So many of the people in the market—the baker, the lady at the fruit stall, lots of people—have given us things and helped us.'

'And you can gift them. You shall make a list and send a gift to each of them.'

Aster had not imagined such a possibility. Maybe there were good things that would come from finding her father.

They went back to the house and found everyone in the main room. Mia had lost her welcoming smile and did not even look up. When she had realised how little of Liana's story she had known, she had been stunned. The twins sensed the shock in the room and ran to Aster, who put her arms around them. Would she now lose these two, her closest connection to her mother?

Mr Chen turned to Kahlid. 'I have upset the household. Perhaps you can help to calm things down.'

They all looked at the king's councillor. He was looking at them and thinking what a challenge it was going to be for all of them, especially for Aster.

'Madame Mia,' he began, 'this is a shock for you, but we will work to find a solution that is acceptable. I do not know at this point exactly what will be arranged, but the king will wish to make sure that you and Aster's sisters are well provided for and that Aster does not lose touch with any of you.'

'I thank you, sir,' Mia managed. She had regained a bit of strength.

Kahlid relieved Aster's mind when he said he would not take her away at the moment. He would give her a chance to think what was best and return the next day to learn her decision. 'We do not have long,' he said, 'because people have seen the carriage. Also wild rumours about yesterday are afloat across the city.'

Kahlid and Mr Chen spoke with Aster about possible options.

'Living in the royal apartment is preferable', Mr Chen pointed out, 'as you have much to learn—more than you can presently imagine. There you will be greatly supported, and I'm sure it will turn out to be best.'

'I think we could move slowly,' Kahlid said, 'but we must work towards living with the king. Will you think about it and talk to me tomorrow?'

Aster only managed a whispered yes. She looked so sad, so worried. Mr Chen, who had risen to go, turned back and put his hand on her shoulder. 'Aster, think about moving slowly. Let's find a temporary home for you while you get to know your father.'

'He will not want to know me,' she sighed. The two men turned towards each other with troubled looks.

'He will care more about knowing you than he will about the kingdom,' Kahlid said firmly. Then he moved towards Aster and bowed.

'Princess Dawn, I will return tomorrow to receive your commands.' He left the room and let himself out of the house.

Mr Chen broke the silence left by Kahlid's last words. 'Whether you are called Aster or Dawn, whether you are a princess or not, you have strength, intelligence, and a warm heart. You will work out a way to proceed.'

He too left. There was a fish to prepare for dinner, then the cleaning up. After the twins were in bed, Aster sat with Mia.

'You'll need to live with your father, sweeting,' Mia told her. 'It wouldn't work with me and the two littlies. I can teach you how to be a servant but not how to act when you have them or how to speak to the great ones or even which fork too use.'

Aster said, 'We could learn together.'

'It's not for me.' Mia was firm. 'I could live in the palace with the servants but not with the royals. It's not a life I could manage.'

'I don't think I can either.'

Mia challenged that. 'Yes, you can. It's what you were born to do.'

'Mia, my father scares me.'

'Aster, what about Lia and Loa's father? You'd rather have him?'

Aster sat perfectly still, looking shocked. 'Oh, Aunt Mia, I never thought . . . Uncle Hew . . . poor Lia and Loa.'

That changed something for her. Suddenly, her father didn't seem so scary. Maybe she could meet him again.

She expected to lie awake worrying about her decisions, but she climbed in with her sisters and went to sleep almost immediately.

When Kahlid arrived, he found her looking more cheerful than the day before. Mia kept the twins in the kitchen, while Aster and Kahlid went into the bigger room.

'May I call you Princess Dawn?' he asked.

'Yes,' she agreed, 'but I don't really feel it's me you're talking to.'

'I have come for your commands, Your Highness, but if you will allow me, I have a message from your father.'

Aster felt a giggle rising in her at being addressed as Your Highness, but she suppressed it and just murmured, 'Please tell me.'

'First, he asks for your forgiveness and begs you to let him speak to you in person. He understands that you are wary of meeting him and wonders if you might come with me for just a short visit—perhaps in a different part of the garden. There is a waterfall surrounded by trees which he would love to show you.'

'He will not expect me to stay? I may come home again?'

'Yes, for today, you may do that, but if you want to continue just visiting for short periods, we will have to find somewhere closer where you and your family can stay—perhaps in my home.'

'Uncle Kahlid, it is hard to think of leaving this house,' Aster spoke slowly. 'It is harder to think of living in the palace, but even Aunt Mia says I must do that.'

'Shall we just think of one step at a time?' Kahlid suggested. 'If you agree, I could take you, Mia, and your two sisters to my house tomorrow. We could have a meal there, and then you and I could visit your father. After that, I will bring you all back here.'

Aster was thinking. She knew she would have to take this first step. Whether she said yes or no today, her life had turned upside down, and she had been the one to set the process going.

Kahlid was quietly waiting for her response.

'Thank you,' she said just above a whisper. 'We will do that.'

The next day, Kahlid arrived in a larger carriage; it was pulled by two horses.

Mia, Aster, Lia, and Loa were all in the very best clothes they owned. The twins were frightened of the horses, but once in the carriage, with Mia's arms around Lia and Aster's around Loa, they bubbled with delight. For their aunt and big sister, excitement at the experience was tempered by the unknown future into which they were heading.

They were soon out of Shackville and mingling with other carriages in the varied traffic of the city. They crossed the bridge, passed the royal palace, and then went through open gates into a courtyard. They stopped in front of a huge sprawling building. The middle section was three storeys high, and on either side, long extensions looked to Aster as if they went on forever. Was it bigger than the palace?

One of the servants helped the visitors down, and Kahlid led them to the front door, which was two steps up from the drive. The door opened as they approached. A uniformed man welcomed them.

Kahlid spoke to him, 'Thank you, Caleb. Is her ladyship in the garden room?'

'Yes, sir, and the housekeeper too, sir.'

They went down a hallway of closed doors until they found an open one. They went into what seemed like a garden. It was full of plants—pots on the floor, hanging from the ceiling, and attached to the walls. Two women rose from a bench. One was in a black dress and looked about Mia's age. The other was younger, wearing a pale-green blouse with a long dark-green skirt.

The younger one stepped forward and grabbed Uncle Kahlid's hand. 'Welcome, everyone. Introduce us properly, Kahlid.'

'Yes, my dear.' He turned to those he had brought and, indicating the lady beside him, said, 'This is my wife, the Lady Alysia Aman.' To her, he said, 'These are the Princess Dawn, her Aunt Mia, and Lia and Loa.'

A bit behind the Lady Alysia stood the older woman. Kahlid called her forward. 'This is our housekeeper, Madame Bachi. Madame Mia, I especially wanted you to meet her. After lunch, she will show you around when Princess Dawn and I go to the palace.'

Mia said, 'I am pleased to make your acquaintance, Madame Bachi.'

Before she left the room, the housekeeper replied, 'And I yours. I will enjoy chatting with you this afternoon.'

The twins were starting to explore, and Mia was worried they might break something, but Kahlid's wife reassured her. 'They'll be fine. Children love to play here. Shortly, someone will take them to meet other children.'

She turned to Aster. 'Princess Dawn, I look forward to getting to know you. I hope you will call me Aunt Alysia.'

Aster always took an extra moment to realise she was Princess Dawn, and she was overwhelmed by everything around her, but she managed to reply 'Thank you' with just a brief pause before the added 'Aunt Alysia'.

When a young woman entered, she curtsied to Lady Aman, who greeted her. 'Shari, here are two darlings for you to look after—Lia and Loa. Maybe they will tell you which is which.'

'Thank you, my lady,' Shari said and smiled at the twins, who were watching her. She took a small cloth square out of her pocket, quickly tied it into a shape with a tail, and set it on her wrist. 'Come help me with this mouse,' she said as the mouse shot up to her elbow. She caught it and brought it back. 'Nice mouse, be still.' She stroked it gently until it escaped again.

The twins were charmed. When she suggested there were other things she could show them, they went with her happily.

Mia felt she should go with them, but Kahlid insisted her company was necessary at lunch. 'They will have lunch with some other children. Don't worry about them. Shari will bring them back if they're unhappy.'

Neither Mia nor Aster fully appreciated the lunch. They felt intimidated by the servants who waited on them and anxious about doing the wrong thing. Both copied their hostess carefully, trying to do it right. Kahlid and Alysia appeared not to notice their nervousness, attempted to put them both at ease, and accepted whatever they did.

Madame Bachi returned and took Mia to check on the twins before showing her around.

'Shall we walk to the palace, Princess?' Kahlid asked. 'Or do you want the chaise?'

'Can we walk?' she asked, and he assured her it was close.

Aunt Alysia gave her a light kiss on the cheek. 'When you come back to take the others home, maybe you can meet our children.'

Even though she was unsure of proper behaviour in this elegant household, Aster felt it might be more comfortable than living with her father. 'Uncle Kahlid,' she asked as they walked towards the palace, 'could I live with you rather than my father?'

'Well, Princess Dawn,' he answered, 'you might come for a short while, and you can certainly visit us often, but'—he stood still and took her hand in his—'in the end, I think you must live in the palace with your father.'

She stood and stared at him unhappily. He spoke again. 'The royal family in Riparia is very small. You are the only heir to the throne.'

'What if I had not been found?'

'There are several who claim a distant relationship with the king. None of the claims are strong, and they would tear the country apart fighting. It is important both for you to be seen as your father's daughter and to learn from him.'

A tiny fear crept into her mind. 'You're not going to leave me in the palace today?'

'Princess Dawn,' Kahlid said, 'you can trust me. No one is going to force you to live in the palace. But I will try to make sure you understand how important it is. I will hope you make the decision to at least attempt it.'

They came to the huge front gates. The soldier opened the small gate, and they walked into the grounds. She looked up at the building again. It was wonderful, and she was curious about everything inside it. She had forgotten how big it was—much bigger than Kahlid's home. The gardens covered even more space. How could anyone not want to live here?

Kahlid led her past the area where they had entered before, past the great stairs leading up to the immense front doors, into the beautiful garden, and then down a path between trees. Where it opened up, there was a waterfall, a little grotto, and a grassy area where her father rose and stood uncertainly, waiting.

Something about him seemed so sad that she almost ran to him. She wanted to comfort him, but then she remembered their last meeting. She did not know what she wanted to do.

He spoke, and his voice was full of pain and longing. 'My daughter, I have hurt you—you for whom I have searched, you whom I have desired with all my heart for twelve years. I do not know how to put things right with you. I can only beg you to forgive me and let me into your life.'

He was a human being in pain, and she went to him and put her arms around him. His arms encircled her, and his tears fell on her head.

As Kahlid watched, he felt his own eyes misting. In one way, he thought he should leave them alone, but he had promised to stay with the princess, so he tried to melt into the bushes and remained where he was.

Father and daughter sat on a bench near the grotto. The water fell softly into the small pond and rippled over rocks as it flowed on; the trees dappled the sunlight. Kahlid began to breathe freely again.

Princess Dawn felt comfortable sitting close beside her father. Mr Chen, Uncle Kahlid, and even Aunt Mia thought she should live in the palace; so did the king. If she decided to do that, Mr Chen, Uncle Kahlid, and her father would be happy; Aunt Mia would be proud of her. It did not seem such a hard thing to do. Perhaps . . .

Then the king spoke, 'You must come and meet the queen.'

Princess Dawn vanished. Aster sprang to her feet, and it was almost a scream, 'No. No. She will hate me. She must not see me.'

The king gaped.

Kahlid was quickly at Aster's side and gave her a smile, which he hoped was big enough to swallow all her fears. 'She will love you. She, as well as the king, has longed to find you and helped the king search for you and your mother.'

'How? Oh, no, she would not want my mother to be found.'

Kahlid held her firmly by the shoulders and looked straight into her eyes. 'You may not understand, but she will be as thrilled as your father to have found you. Calm down, Aster. She will be a great support to you. She will be your best friend.'

He sat her back down on the bench by the king. All was still now except for the sound of the water. No one spoke.

When Kahlid thought enough time had passed, he said, 'Princess Dawn, we will be ruled by you. I think you would sleep better tonight if you met the queen before you returned home, but I am quite willing to take you back now or whenever you wish.'

Aster felt so confused. She did not know what she wanted except to return everything to the way it was before. She knew that was impossible. Would the queen really be glad to meet her? It did not seem likely, but Kahlid had proved to be reliable. The king was her father; surely he would not want to take her to the queen if he thought the queen would hate her. She looked at her father. He was sitting slumped beside her with his eyes closed; he looked so sad. Aster reached out and took one of his hands in hers. Rio opened his eyes, looked at his daughter, and put his other hand on top of hers.

Aster swallowed; she trembled inside as she said, 'I will go with you, Father, to meet the queen.'

'Thank you, Dawn,' he said quietly.

All three felt some apprehension as they walked through the garden to the palace and then to the royal apartment, but once the queen was introduced to Princess Dawn, there was no doubt that the king's daughter knew she had found someone who would stand beside her and help her to adjust to her new life and the loss of the old one. She began the process of thinking of herself as Princess Dawn and letting Aster go.

Chapter 8

Soora understood much of what Dawn was feeling and would face in the days ahead. As well, hers was a lonely life, and she still missed the sisters with whom she had lived before she went to Riparia. She was truly delighted to meet Rio's daughter, a girl who would share in the life of the royal family. She showed Dawn around the royal apartment and even took her to her favourite spot, which overlooked a small private section of the garden. Soora tied a colourful little scarf around Dawn's neck and said how much fun they would both have choosing new clothes for her. There was lots of talking, and the king and queen were eager to learn about her life as Aster. Tea was served in royal style by a maidservant.

When Kahlid suggested he and Princess Dawn needed to go, the queen asked the question neither of the men would have dared, 'Dawn, I hate to have you leave at all. When are you coming to stay for good?'

The princess had known that living in the royal palace was something everyone expected her to do, but she had not considered a specific time for this to happen. She did not know what to say. She looked at Kahlid.

'Princess Dawn has not set a date,' he said, 'but she cannot stay much longer in Shackville–only a few days at the most.'

The queen was horrified. 'She's not going there—surely not.'

Kahlid assured the queen that guards would be in place at the house and all would be well. 'The house she lives in is well built and spacious, and there are things she will want to bring with her. She needs to go back.'

'Then, which day will you come?' She smiled at Dawn.

Kahlid came to the rescue again. 'We will see,' he said. 'She may not feel able to separate from her family immediately. I will let you know.'

Suddenly, Dawn felt herself embraced by the queen. 'I will count the minutes until you come,' she whispered and kissed the princess lightly on the cheek. Her father hugged and kissed her as well. She was reminded of how much she had loved her mother's hugs and kisses.

Dawn felt she did not express thanks properly to the queen or to her father, but she would see them again—she could even look forward to that—and she would tell them of her gratitude then.

She and Kahlid had passed through the gate and were nearly to his house when she asked, 'Do I truly have to be out of the house in a few days?'

'Yes. I'm sorry, but now that it will become known that you are the king's daughter, we have decided we cannot leave you there.'

'Mia and the twins—can they stay?'

'No. If Mia likes the set-up in my home, they can move there. If not, she can stay with us for a while until we can organise something else.'

'The palace has lots of rooms,' she said wistfully.

'Yes, there is space for an army,' he agreed, 'but we cannot put someone with whom you wish to have a close relationship in the servants' wing, and Mia would not be comfortable anywhere else.'

She was Dawn, the daughter of the king. When she was Aster, a Shackville child, she thought she could go anywhere, but she could not go into the palace or the homes of people like Kahlid or ride in a chaise. She did not even know who her father was. Now the view of the future was unclear, and it seemed there would be different places she could not go; it seemed there would be many places she could not go by herself. On the other hand, she was beginning to realise that there were exciting experiences awaiting her, and every time she thought of the queen, she felt enveloped in a smile.

Mia had enjoyed her afternoon with Madame Bachi. Lia and Loa had romped delightedly through their time with other children. When Kahlid discussed her options with Madame Mia, she had no doubt that life in the Aman household would suit them well. She would take over as seamstress, a job that was vacant. Under the housekeeper, she would be responsible for mending and sewing. She and the twins would have two connecting rooms near the common dining area, where meals would be provided. Lia and Loa would attend the school Kahlid and Alysia provided for their servants' children.

They would be close to the palace and could keep in touch with Aster—or Dawn, as she was now to be known.

Kahlid was well satisfied with arrangements for everyone except the princess. After speaking with Mia, he found the twelve-year-old in happy conversation with his wife. As he entered the room, he heard Dawn say words which gave him hope, 'She was so wonderful. The queen treated me as if I was her own daughter.'

He sat down beside his wife.

'Is it time to go?' Dawn asked.

'Yes, but I want to ask you a question. As I told you, soon you will have to move out of Shackville and settle somewhere, either permanently or as a place to visit while you think further. It may be impossible for you to make a final choice quickly. I wondered what you would think of joining the king and queen for a week away from the palace. There're a couple of places where your father used to take your mother in order to have a break from palace protocol. It could be understood that you were coming back to spend time with Mia and your sisters after a week.'

When the princess did not answer immediately, Alysia said, 'Maybe Dawn could think about it overnight.'

When they returned to Shackville, the small family began to gather items to take with them into their new lives. They did not own many clothes or have many possessions. There were a couple of books that Liana had brought into the house, but pictures and ornaments were not part of their lives. Mia had herself embroidered covers for the back and seat of a chair she would take with her, but most of the furniture would remain in the house. Even though it was situated in Shackville, Kahlid hoped to find someone to occupy it and give Mia an income. Meanwhile, Aziz, one of the royal guards, would be stationed there with his wife and two boys, who were guards in training.

Mia, Dawn, and the twins shared a light meal with them.

Lia and Loa were put to bed; Aziz and his family settled in the extra rooms Hew had built when he married Dawn's mother. Mia and Dawn stood together, looking over everything.

'What are you going to do, Aster—uh, Dawn—when we leave here?' Mia asked.

'Maybe I will go with my father and Queen Soora.'

Mia was surprised. 'Move straight to the palace?'

'No, not that,' Dawn told her. 'Uncle Kahlid suggested they'd take me somewhere away from the palace for a week. After that, I'd come see you and the twins.'

Mia smiled. 'Kahlid has good ideas. Will you do that?'

'I'll think about it.'

After Dawn climbed into bed with the twins, she did. But it wasn't long before she'd made a decision. She was no longer so scared of her father, but the stronger influence—although she did not realise it—was the way Soora filled the deep hole left by her mother's death. She would try Kahlid's plan. She fell asleep with happy thoughts of Soora.

When the day came to leave Shackville, Dawn was not sure how she felt. There was sadness in leaving the place where she and her mother had lived together. Now she would not see even Aunt Mia or the twins every day.

Also Mr Chen, her constant support, said he might be unable to visit her in the palace. 'Your father may be angry with me for not telling him where you and your mother were.'

'Why?' she asked. 'He had another wife.'

'Yes, that was your mother's fear. It is hard to see how he would have managed if he had discovered where your mother was. But even when your mother died, I did nothing.'

'But . . . but, Mr Chen, I need you. I cannot lose you.'

'You will not,' he said. 'If we cannot meet in the palace, I will see you at Kahlid's. You'll see him often. Just tell him when you want to see me.'

'But I have much more to learn. I need to see my teacher almost every day.' Dawn was distraught.

'We will have to wait and see what is possible. It will work out,' he assured her.

Dawn was also excited by what the future might bring, but that excitement was always limited by anxiety. So much was unknown, and she was moving into a completely different world. As they rode in the open carriage towards the Aman mansion, she tightly grasped the basket which held her clothes for the week ahead. They were not those of a princess, but she was not at the moment, going to the palace.

They arrived at Uncle Kahlid and Aunt Alysia's house. Dawn went with Mia and the twins to see their accommodation. She hugged and kissed each of them.

'I'll be back in a week,' she told them.

All four of them stood with their host and hostess just outside the front door to watch the royal carriage arrive.

It was a splendid sight. The four horses pulling the large closed carriage were in top condition with well-brushed, gleaming white coats; each had a dancing plume on its head. The carriage was black with elaborate gold decorations, including a large *R* and *S* for the reigning king and queen; it was as shiny as a mirror. Two servants in royal livery sat on the open seat at the front, and two stood on the back.

The king got out and led Dawn to the carriage. One of the servants took her basket and helped her up on to the step. She took another step up, and there was Queen Soora, smiling and eager to hug her. She waved to those whom she was leaving. She felt strange, as if she was playing a part in a fairy story. But it was a true story—exciting and frightening.

The whole trip in the royal carriage was a surprise to the princess. She was amazed at the interior, which was a complete contrast to the simple benches of the carriages in which Kahlid had transported her. It was not just that it was closed in and larger, but it had long cushions on the seats and some smaller ones which could be put behind you or under your head.

It was, of course, harder to see all that was outside, but rain would not get in or the dust of the road. It still bounced about while going over the rough roads, but the speed was thrilling. She had never gone so fast before.

It was not possible to carry on a conversation, and she wondered how the two coachmen at the back could hold on. But she was travelling in a royal carriage with a real king and queen. She was in a wonderful story which she could enjoy more fully than if she had been hunting for the right words to say.

When they stopped and got out, it was in a grassy area where two willows framed a view of the river, which flowed close by. She had never seen the river except where it passed through the city and could hardly stop admiring it. The servants brought food to them, but the princess was much more delighted by a mother swan and its cygnet floating peacefully by as she and the others ate their meal.

The next time they stopped, they had reached Riverwood Cottage, one of the places where Rio, when he was the prince, had spent time with his beloved Amethyst. It looked as though it belonged in a fairy story with its turf roof, tiny windows, and twisting path.

The door stood open, and a young woman emerged and curtsied to the queen. 'Welcome, Your Majesty, all is ready as you requested.' Dawn was particularly impressed with the curtsy, which she did not imagine she could ever learn to do as expertly.

Inside, the rooms were small, but everything was bright and colourful. There were pictures on the walls, curtains at every window, rugs on the floors. Dawn thought the largest rug in the main room looked like a magic carpet.

'Come see your room,' Soora called. She showed Dawn into a small one with flowered curtains and left her to investigate. The bedspread looked as though a hundred butterflies had landed on it. Beside the bed was a little rug—the skin of a woolly animal. Dawn slipped out of her sandals and wiggled her toes in it, enjoying the warm softness. Outside the tiny window, she could see huge trees and the glint of water not too far away. The pictures on the walls were all of fairies and wood sprites dancing and playing amid flowers and trees. There was a bookshelf with a small collection of books and a few beautiful little trinkets which fascinated her.

Soora returned with the maid, whom she introduced as Ryana. Before handing Dawn her basket, she made her perfect curtsy to the princess. 'I am so happy to meet you, Your Highness. May your stay be full of joy.'

The princess managed an 'I thank you' but wondered if she would ever get used to being addressed as Your Highness.

Then her father called them to go outside for a look at the garden. There were pansies and hollyhocks, geraniums, and asters. There were colourful flowers blooming on every side of the house. When they walked towards the river, there were shy bits of colour peeping from the grasses and blooms on the bushes. And there was the river. Rocks, ferns, and grasses filled the banks, and there were a few water lilies in a nearly still section away from the main flow.

As they walked back, the queen asked Dawn to go with her to see something in the royal bedchamber. The princess went gladly; today there seemed to be a delightful surprise around every corner. When they entered the room, Soora showed her first a nightgown and matching dressing gown in soft pink and then a simple sheath in blues and purples.

'They're for you, if you like them,' the queen said. 'Later you can choose for yourself, and the royal dressmaker will make whatever you wish.'

Dawn stared in wonder. She had never seen anything like these garments. The materials seemed too beautiful to wear. The queen helped her put on the dress and then tied a ribbon for a belt and put a matching bit of ribbon in her hair. When Dawn looked in the mirror, she did not recognise the person who looked back at her.

'Would you like to show your father?' Soora asked.

Dawn wasn't sure. She felt afraid to move anywhere in the dress, but it seemed as though showing her father might be fun. 'If you come with me,' she said.

'Of course.'

They went back together. The colours in the dress seemed to emphasise Dawn's eyes, which were so like her mother's.

'Ah,' the king breathed, 'you are always beautiful to me. In that dress, you also remind me of your mother. It is so, so wonderful to have you here, Dawn.'

'Thank you . . . Father.' She had to remind herself to call him father, but it gave her a lovely, bubbly feeling inside.

As they were changing her back into the clothes she had been wearing, Soora asked, 'What would you like to call me, Dawn? I'm not your mother, but I'd like to be your friend. Do you want to call me Soora or Aunt Soora, or do you prefer something else?'

She felt shy with this lovely and elegant woman whom she was beginning to think of as a fairy godmother, but she managed to respond, 'I'd like to call you Soora, if you're happy with that.'

'Wonderful—we'll be good friends.'

With only Ryana to serve them—the coach and the four liveried servants had vanished (as they do in fairy tales)—the meal was more casual than lunch at Kahlid's had been. Dawn knew, of course, that life in the palace could turn out to be even more formal than the Aman household, but she enjoyed her Riverwood Cottage time. She had not quite relaxed; there was still tenseness, uncertainty, but her two companions seemed to want nothing more than to make her happy.

After dinner, they took a short stroll outside around the cottage, but Dawn was beginning to droop. Back in her bedroom, the new nightgown made her eyes open wide in delight, but she was soon tucked into bed. When the king went in to kiss her goodnight, she was already asleep.

It had all been so wonderful. It had been like riding on the crest of a wave that just built and built. She had gone to sleep with a feeling of immense wonder and amazement that she seemed to have arrived in this place, a place to which it was possible that everything in her life had been heading. But when she woke in the morning, shortly before the sun rose, it seemed as though the wave had dumped her down roughly on a rocky beach.

She was alone in a bed with no twins. There was no Aunt Mia. She was in a lovely cottage to be sure, but there were only strangers here. They had given her a fabulous day, but she did not belong with them. She was almost as bereft as when her mother died.

She lay in bed and studied the room in the dim light. There were the pictures and the bookshelves she had noticed last night. There was the soft little rug by the bed and the tiny window which looked out on the garden and the path to the river. Why did she long for the bare room she had shared with Lia and Loa, its cracked walls, its window with no view?

She felt sobs rising. There were tears in her eyes. She brushed them away with the back of her hand and sat up. Outside she could see trees, their trunks and leaves brightening splendidly as the sun rose. She thought she would not mind hiding there among the plants—the small trees and bushes which could shelter her and the giant trees which rose so tall and magnificent and held it all together. She heard a bird calling; it seemed to pause, waiting for a reply, and then called again. But there was still no reply from its own kind. Here in this place, it was the same for her.

There was a soft rap on the door. It opened, and the man who called himself her father stood there. 'May I come in?'

She nodded, and he went to the soft rug and stood just out of reach. 'It is strange for you to wake up here.' His smile was hardly a smile. 'Are you missing your aunt and your sisters?'

Tears flooded her eyes and fell on to the covers. He went to her, put his arms around her, and held her as she sobbed. He understood, and he cared. He was really her father. When she finished crying and looked up at him, she saw he had tears in his eyes.

He gave her a handkerchief. As she wiped her eyes, she seemed to wipe away some of the sadness that had filled her. He loosened his arms but gave her a gentle squeeze. 'You will see the family you are missing soon again. I hope it won't be long before you feel we're family too.'

Soora, wrapped in an elegant dressing gown, came in, picked up Dawn's dressing gown, and suggested she put it on and go to breakfast. 'We don't do this in the palace.' She smiled. 'But we can here.'

It was a quieter day than the one before. There was time for talking and listening. When the king reminisced about coming to Riverwood with Amethyst, Soora noticed Dawn's confusion and embarrassment.

'It's all right,' she said. 'Perhaps we need to help you to understand. Will you explain, Rio?'

'It's better coming from you,' he suggested.

They sat on a bench by the river. The queen's first words were 'Your father never stopped loving your mother.'

Dawn looked at her father. 'That's true,' he said.

'But . . .' Dawn was confused.

The queen put her hand on one of Dawn's. 'We are married. We went through all the ceremony the old king arranged. But we have never considered ourselves married. I did not wish to be married at all, and your father was already married and did not wish to marry me. We felt betrayed by the formal treaty made between our fathers.'

She paused. The river rippled by, sparkling in the sun. Fluffy clouds sat in a blue sky. Dawn did not look at either Soora or Rio.

When Soora continued, she explained how they had talked it over and decided that the kingdom needed its king and queen—at that time, its prince and princess as heirs to the throne—but that for them this would be only a formal arrangement where they would appear in public and fulfil their responsibilities together. Rio planned to continue to live with Amethyst.

'How could he do that?' Dawn asked.

'I think he probably could not have managed,' the queen said, 'but we were young and desperate. Only your mother was thinking clearly.'

The king cleared his throat. 'We must all thank Amethyst . . .' But he could not continue.

Dawn was perplexed. Had her mother been sent away by the old king or maybe by the present king? Had they treated her mother badly?

Much of the rest of the day was spent with the three of them talking together. Eventually, she understood that her mother had been the one to show not only the greatest wisdom but also the greatest courage in a situation that could have ended up even more unhappily.

'Your mother acted without telling anyone. She did it for me and the kingdom,' her father told her, 'but most of all, she did it for you. She did not want you to grow up feeling the disdain of the ruling king and queen, who were your grandparents.'

Would her mother have told her all this if she had been alive when her daughter turned twelve? Dawn wondered about that as she lay in bed that night. She thought Liana would have found it a hard story to tell.

She did not think her mother would have taken her to the palace and asked to see the king. She was uncertain about whether or not her mother would even have been willing to tell her that the king was her father. Yet when Liana was dying, she had stressed that Aster—as she was then—must wear the pendant, keep it always round her neck. So her mother did want her to find her father; she wanted her daughter to live in the palace with the king.

As Dawn settled down, she thought of how many people there were who wanted her to take her proper place as the princess and live in the palace. Soon she fell asleep.

Chapter 9

When the princess woke, the sun was shining, and she felt as though her mother was with her in this place where Rio and Amethyst had been happy together. Her mother seemed to be at her shoulder—proud of her and encouraging her to be the best princess she could be.

She dressed quickly. As she walked through the main room, she greeted Ryana, who was setting up breakfast. Dawn let herself out into the garden and laughed at a startled rabbit who thought he had it all to himself. She breathed in deeply and listened hard—what sounds could she hear? There was a bird singing somewhere towards the river, and she thought she could hear the river itself. But there was something deeper, something within. She seemed to hear her mother's voice, soft and comforting, saying, 'My lovely Aster.' Once long, long ago, when she was a baby, her mother would have called her Dawn.

After a while, she went inside and got Ryana to help her set up the breakfast in a sunny spot by the house. Soora and her father were delighted, especially with Dawn taking the initiative.

During the morning, she told them about Liana, the mother who had cared for her and tried to prepare her for life, whatever it might bring. Rio hung on every word and was not too upset by Liana's marriage when he learned that she did not even like Hew but married him only to secure a home for herself and her daughter.

Soora brightened Dawn's day when she said, 'What an amazing mother. You were surely the lucky one. I could never have managed what she did.'

At lunch, Ryana said there would be a clown and a performance by a group of local singers that afternoon at the country fair nearby. Soora suggested they go to the tiny hamlet, dressed simply and without the coach. It wasn't far to walk and two of the coachmen—not in their livery—could accompany them to help, if necessary, and to carry parcels. Ryana could go as well.

It was fun with the six of them walking along the road together. Maybe no one would recognise the king, and they could just be travellers visiting a country fair. At first, that seemed to be working. It reminded Dawn of her market except that there were fewer people, and they were not boisterous but polite, treating them as welcome strangers. Everyone moved about, sharing smiles and greetings.

She was enjoying the afternoon when she heard a harsh, nasal voice, 'Well met, cousin Rio, and who are all your companions?'

She turned to see a young man with a facial expression that reminded her of Hew, putting his hand on her father's shoulder.

Her father was scowling; he shrugged the offending hand off. Soora stepped forward and spoke softly to the transgressor. She seemed to know him but was suggesting that he move away.

He kept his place. 'Who are these lovely damsels?' he asked, pointing to Dawn and Ryana. The king nodded at the coachmen, grabbed Soora and Dawn, and turned abruptly. The coachmen stopped the man moving towards them. The royal family and Ryana moved out of the crowd and hurried towards Riverwood Cottage.

'Who was that man?' Dawn asked when they slowed down.

'He's Durand Scrope,' her father answered, 'the more unsavoury of the two main pretenders to the throne of Riparia.'

'He's related to us?' she asked.

'Not that anyone can demonstrate,' Soora said. 'He thinks if he says it loud enough and often enough, it will be true.'

The king explained that as there was no visible heir to the throne, several claimants had surfaced, but he thought only two were serious. The second one was Frederick, the son of one of the counsellors who was a distant relation. He was a handsome and pleasant young man with little ambition, but his father had put him forward as the right choice for the kingdom.

'You were always the heir,' Rio said, 'and now we've found you, hopefully others will fade away.'

'Oh,' Dawn exclaimed, 'that's one of the reasons Kahlid said I need to live in the palace.'

'It would certainly be a good idea,' her father agreed.

That night, her father asked her if there was anything at all he could do to make it easier for her to move to the palace. Dawn was quiet for a few moments and then she said, 'Yes.'

'What is it?'

'Bring Mr Chen back to live in the garden cottage'.

Soora looked up with interest, and Dawn held her breath. The king looked serious for a few moments, and then he smiled. 'Things always did seem to run smoother when Professor Chen was in residence,' he said. 'Do you think he would come?'

'I think so. He would be so happy that you are not angry with him.'

'Aha, did he think I was angry? Well, he was correct, but how could I be angry if my beautiful daughter was willing to live with us in the palace?'

When the week was over, Dawn spent three delightful days with Mia and the twins. They had lots to tell her, and she was full of stories about her time at Riverwood Cottage.

Then she moved from the vibrant Aman household into the palace. It was much more difficult than she had imagined.

The palace was immense. When Kahlid walked there with her, they passed the long wing where Kahlid's office and other rooms were located. It seemed very long ago when she had sat there. Kahlid told her the guards were also based in that wing; some even lived there. Next, Kahlid pointed out the huge central section where the grand front steps descended to the drive.

'There's a ballroom which, with its supplementary rooms, is as big as a good-sized house and a dining room that seats over 100 people,' he told her. 'Then there are the elaborate kitchens and storerooms for all the china, glassware, and cutlery.'

Dawn wondered how she could ever manage to find her way. It was much more complicated than the whole of Shackville. 'Where did my mother live?' she asked.

'At the back. Behind and above the kitchens and formal rooms, there's a large area set aside for servants who live in the palace,' Kahlid answered. 'There are a few small flats for the more-senior ones. Your grandmother was head housekeeper, so your mother grew up in one of those flats.' He continued as they moved on, 'Later she lived with your father in a ground-floor apartment. Its entrance is just round those next lot of bushes.'

They came to a door by which they entered the palace. Inside was a large entrance area, the walls hung with beautiful tapestries. There were the steps which led up to the royal apartment. When they reached its door, two footmen bowed and opened it. Her father and Soora welcomed them with smiles and hugs.

Kahlid left, but she felt fairly comfortable. She had been here before and the apartment itself, while large, was tiny compared to the whole palace. It was a safe space. Soora and her father were known, and her love for both of them was growing.

However, her comfort gradually leaked away. When a maid came into the room, Dawn looked at her and saw someone close to her own age who might be a friend, but the maid put up a barrier with a curtsy and 'Welcome, Your Highness'. Maids and footmen were eager to please, to do whatever she wanted, except they could not be friends. They bowed and curtsied, and she was unable to engage them in conversation.

It was a settling-in day. Her father and Soora took her walking in the garden and showed her the outside of the far end of the palace, beyond where she and Kahlid had walked. The queen made sure Dawn knew how to get back and forth from the apartment to the garden by herself. She also showed the girl the end of the royal corridor and spoke of the delights she could see there another day.

Most of it was pleasant, but somehow she felt she was in a glass bubble where only Soora and her father could join her.

When she awoke the following morning, she longed for Mia, Lia, and Loa. She asked if she might visit them. She knew that it was only a short walk. Soora offered to go with her. 'I'd love to have a chance to speak with Mia', she said, 'and get to know the twins. I only saw them from a distance before.'

She was glad of the queen's company. She might not have been sure of the way, and she would have felt awkward on her own with the footman, apparently required to accompany them if she or Soora walked outside the palace grounds.

When they arrived at Kahlid's, both he and Alysia were at the front door, welcoming their niece Kara, who had arrived for a ten-day visit. She was seventeen and the daughter of Kahlid's brother, who was also one of the king's counsellors. She knew Soora well and was delighted to meet the princess for whom the whole country had been searching when Kara was a small child. For Dawn, it was almost a magical encounter; Kara was the first young person she had met who was not a servant but a member of a family that was part of the court. As well as that, both she and Kara felt relaxed together almost from the start. Dawn was even reluctant to rush off to see her family. How would she find Kara again once she left?

But everyone else was aware of why the princess had come. Alysia was soon asking one of the maids to show her where Mia and the twins were. Soora decided to stay with the others, and Dawn went off to find the three she missed so much.

The queen had noticed the princess's delight when she met and talked with Kara. Her eyes had sparkled, and her smile had seemed more enveloping than usual. She wondered, 'Kara, is there any way I could entice you to spend your ten days in the city with us in the palace—or at least some of it?'

'That's generous of you, Your Majesty,' Kara replied.

'I think Dawn would be greatly helped', Soora continued, 'by someone your age showing her around the building, helping her to choose new clothes, and just being a friend. I suspect she has found even the first night lonely.'

Alysia spoke, 'Although we'd be the losers, I think your idea is perfect, Soora. It's just what Dawn needs—and right away, before she gets despondent. What about it, Kara?'

'It'd be fun. Do I get to live in the royal apartment?

She was impressed when the queen said, 'Yes, of course.'

When Dawn was ready to go back to the palace, she found not only Soora but also Kara ready to go with her. The footman had gone; Kara's things were in the carriage, which waited for the three of them. The princess felt like dancing; she would have ten days with a person close to her age who could be a friend and knew her way around the palace and all the confusing procedures of court life.

It was a happy time for the king's daughter. Kara took Dawn on a new tour every day. First, they went out into the royal corridor, which had been Amethyst's favourite place when she was a child. It ended at the royal apartment, so it was easy to find, and Dawn knew she would go there often in the future.

The first time took her breath away. There was so much to see. There were portraits—many of them of her relatives; there were beautiful pieces of furniture, cabinets full of fascinating carvings and jewels, and the doll house. When Kara told her the story of Rio having it brought to the rooms where he and her mother were living, the story of Amethyst dusting the pieces of furniture and playing with it as she wished, Dawn was not sure if it was fact or imagination. She looked hard at it and tried to imagine her mother reorganising it all.

On the way back, they stopped at the library. In its way, it was even more amazing—so many books. She had not imagined there could be so many, certainly not in one place.

By the time Kara left, Dawn no longer felt confined to the apartment. She knew her way around. As well, Kara had filled in a lot of bits of information she would have learned without trying if she had been brought up as a princess. With Kara's help, she had chosen materials, and the royal seamstress was preparing a whole new wardrobe for her.

Mr Chen was to arrive a few days after Kara left. Ever since Dawn's mother had died—and even before that—he had been her main source of strength and support. She knew that if her tutor and friend was available, she would be able to fill her role as princess and probably even as future queen. Without him, she could not see how she would manage.

The garden cottage was already well prepared by others, but she wanted to do something herself for Mr Chen. She thought of flowers, and she knew that all she had to do was to mention the idea and probably several people would rush to get them for her. But she wanted to do it all by herself with her own hands.

So just after the sun rose, before anyone was there to stop or help her, she left the apartment quietly and went into the garden to pick a bouquet of flowers. After she picked them, she went to the cottage. Luckily, no one had noticed her yet.

She found a container and tried different ways of arranging them until she was satisfied; then she set them in the middle of the table with a note. '*Welcome*, Mr Chen. I picked these myself because I am so glad you are here. With love . . .' She almost signed it Aster but remembered and wrote, 'Princess Dawn'.

At the door, she stopped and looked back, pleased to have done something herself for Mr Chen.

It was a great help for Dawn to have her tutor living in the royal precinct. He was a bridge between two worlds which had little in common. He was a well known and solid support from her time in Shackville; he had known her mother well. He was also comfortable in the palace and knowledgeable about things Dawn might need to learn as heir to the throne of Riparia.

She did not really like to think about that future. But Mr Chen gently encouraged her, and because he was there to support her, she was able to work towards what seemed a daunting and thoroughly frightening situation to the young princess.

In the mornings, as she walked through the gardens to her lessons, Dawn felt it was almost like returning to the happy times before her mother's death.

Her lessons now were a mixture of the learning in which any advanced student might engage and instructions in palace protocol. She also was able to ask about the things that troubled her, whatever she found odd. Her sessions with Mr Chen did more to help her adjust to her new life than anything else that could have been suggested.

Another good thing that happened was that her father and Mr Chen had a long talk. The tutor explained how he had been guided by Amethyst and the concern they both had for the welfare of the princess and also the kingdom.

The king, always partial to Amethyst's ideas, eventually realised what a huge service Professor Chen had done for the kingdom in teaching and watching over the princess while she was in Shackville. He embraced the tutor with his former warmth and often visited him in the garden cottage. For Rio, it became one of his favourite ways to relax, and he often gained insights into the daughter whom he had only recently come to know.

Dawn felt much better about her new life, but sometimes there was still a loneliness which sent her to the garden, where she could find something she had not seen before or just relax in the peaceful atmosphere away from the formality within the palace.

The gardeners were mostly young and more ready than the indoor servants to speak with her, at least about the plants and the work they were doing. They still addressed her as Your Highness and bowed too much for her liking—all except for one of them.

He was tall and slim, his hair was red brown and tended to curl, and his nose reminded her of her mother's. His name was Maren. He addressed her as Princess or Princess Dawn. While he was always polite, he seemed to speak to her as if they were of equal status; he did not hold himself apart—in a different social class—as she felt the others did. Often he forgot to bow, which delighted her.

Dawn began to look forward to finding him when she went to the garden. Where before she had stopped to speak to whatever gardeners she saw, she now kept wandering unless she happened on Maren; if not, she enjoyed her walk without stopping to ask questions.

She spent a lot of time in the garden—not only roaming around the pathways, but also working in the pergola on the tasks her tutor assigned. For her, it was a better place to think than inside the palace, where she found maids and footmen disturbing. Also, she never knew when Maren might turn up.

Being a princess could be hard, but it grew easier as she became familiar with her new life and with the families of the court. Soora arranged small dinners to introduce her to them and, every so often, invited a few girls or young women to spend an afternoon at the palace. As well as Kara, there were others with whom she formed friendships. If, even over time, there was no one besides Kara who stood out as special for her, she was well liked and enjoyed these occasions.

She was friendly herself and liked being with people—all except for one person, Durand Scrope.

When he had appeared at the fair near Riverwood Cottage, he had not made a good impression. It only got worse. Next he had come, uninvited, to the first dinner Soora had given for her. Only two counsellor families had been invited—Kahlid and Alysia (without their children, who were too young) and Counsellor Pound with his wife, their daughter, and Frederick, their son, one of the two main pretenders to the throne.

Just after those guests had arrived, before they went in to dinner, Durand Scrope had entered the room. Dawn thought that her father had been about to eject him when the queen moved forward and greeted him, 'A bit unexpected to see you tonight. I had you down for another evening, but now you're here . . .'

Later she explained to the princess that she had been planning not to invite him at all but thought it was better to let him stay than to throw him out. She would certainly not include him in any further invitations.

When they went in to dinner, Soora had Frederick escort Dawn. She was seated on her father's right, with Durand as far away as possible, in the place of honour on the queen's right. Although he attempted to speak with the princess after dinner, Kahlid moved him on, and he only managed the briefest of remarks.

However, Durand was determined. No snub, rebuff, or being ignored had any effect. She was glad she did not see him often, but over the years, on the occasion of any official function, he would appear and keep as close to Dawn as he could. Sometimes he was present when she was invited to visit the families she had met. He was adept at weaselling his way into her company, and she disliked him more each time.

His nasal voice made her nauseous. He tended to put his hand on her arm, and she felt cheapened by his touch. The overcomplimentary ways he addressed her—'most glorious and gorgeous beauty' or 'star that lights my world'—seemed insulting to her.

He spoke and acted as though there was some relationship between them, and his manner became more and more forward.

When he was not there, she forgot him as she began to fit more comfortably into her new life. She visited Mia and the twins weekly, and they went to her almost as often. As they grew older, it became more and more fun to show the garden and the palace to the twins—and good for them. Even by the time they turned ten, they knew the names of many of the plants in the garden and had picked up bits of history without trying through visits to the royal corridor.

Chapter 10

After living in the palace for a full six years, Dawn was truly part of the community, and yet she still felt a certain separateness. She accepted that as a reality; she was not from their world. She understood why she felt instant warmth towards the servants who surrounded her although their manner towards her would never permit any relationship to develop—except with Maren. She often met him in the garden, and speaking with him always brightened her day. There was something about him which made her think that he could understand both her worlds and accept them both. Mr Chen was the only other person who had that ability.

One day when she was in the pergola, puzzling over some particularly difficult mathematics her tutor seemed to have assigned to point out her limits, she saw Maren nearby. That was all the excuse she needed to let the complex problems go for a bit.

'Good afternoon, Maren,' she called, 'are you planting something new?'

'No, Princess,' he said, 'just weeding.' He went to the pergola. 'What are you doing there?'

'It's more what I'm not doing. I can't get it straight.'

'Maybe I can help.' He looked down at the figures on the page for a few moments.

Dawn wished she had just put it away. She didn't want him to be embarrassed by finding he couldn't do it either, but she needn't have worried.

'Here, let me show you,' he said. 'It's not hard once you get the trick.'

He looked awkward leaning over. 'Please sit, Maren. Can you really do it?'

He sat and showed her slowly and patiently, then watched her do one of the problems herself. She had a big smile, 'It works! Oh, thank you, but I've taken you away from your work.'

'I'll just have to work a bit faster,' he said and returned to the weeding.

When she took her work to her lesson the next day and told Mr Chen how she had managed to do it, he was amazed. 'One of the gardeners knew how to do that? You're not making up stories, Princess? No one hired as a gardener would have anywhere near the education.'

She insisted that Maren had indeed shown her how. 'It seemed easy for him.'

That afternoon, the tutor wandered out to the shed where the head gardener held sway. 'Do you think you could lend me that young chap Maren?' he asked Brad. 'I'd like just a couple of things done a certain way at the cottage.'

'How'd you know which was the best of the boys, Professor?' Brad asked. 'I could let you have two of the others, and you'd be worse off.'

'I'd be obliged if you'd let me have Maren.'

'Seeing it's you, Professor,' he agreed, 'I'll have him up there first thing in the morning.'

'Afternoon'd be preferable, if it's all right with you.'

'Tomorrow afternoon,' Brad promised.

When Maren turned up at the cottage, the professor asked him to come inside. 'You can leave your tools on the steps,' he suggested.

'You've got a plan for the work?' Maren asked.

When they were both inside, Professor Chen asked Maren to sit down and admitted, 'I'm afraid I got you here on false pretences, Maren. Princess Dawn told me about how you helped her.'

'I'm sorry, sir, if I should not have done that.'

'Oh, it's perfectly fine. No objection, but I was curious. Do you think any of the other gardeners could have done those mathematical problems?'

'Perhaps not.' Maren wondered where this was going.

'Absolutely not, I'd say' was the professor's assessment. 'Do you have an objection to telling me where you learned advanced mathematics of that sort?'

'I'd rather not.'

The professor switched his tactics, moving the conversation into geography, history, and philosophy. He even discovered Maren's facility with languages and came to a conclusion, which greatly intrigued him, that Riparian was not his mother tongue. Maren was there for the whole afternoon, by which time the tutor had established that the young gardener's knowledge extended into many fields and even possibly exceeded the king's in some of them.

As Maren was about to leave, Professor Chen asked, 'Do you have any interest in further study or teaching?'

Maren smiled. 'Interest, of course, not likely at the moment. But I've really enjoyed the afternoon. Fascinating to talk to you, Professor, worth it, even if Brad doesn't think I've done a full day's work.'

'Might be best at the moment if we don't say too much to Brad. Just tell him you did what I asked, but it didn't improve the garden. You'd be willing to go further with study if it's paid?'

Maren was confused by the conversation but agreed that he'd be glad to study if it fit with his responsibilities.

Shortly after the young gardener left, the tutor sent a message to the king by one of the footmen. He requested a meeting. Instead of a reply as to when the tutor might see him in the palace, the king, who enjoyed visiting the cottage, turned up after the evening meal to be met by the professor's first question: 'Rio, can you think of any young men who would have the makings of the best sort of counsellor for Dawn when she becomes queen?'

The king's silence was followed by 'Well, no, I don't think so'.

'I don't know of any among the court I'd particularly recommend myself,' said Professor Chen, 'but one of your team of gardeners could qualify.'

'Chen, are you getting weak in the brain, or is my hearing failing? I thought you said a gardener could become a counsellor for my daughter.'

'I did, Your Majesty,' the tutor said, using the title to emphasise his point.

Rio just looked at him and wondered what the punch line would be.

After a moment, Professor Chen started to explain about Maren. 'I got him to come to see me because I was intrigued that he could do the problems I'd given Dawn. I hadn't shown her how to do them. I wanted to see how she would approach something that was beyond what she had learned. They were not easy.'

'Well,' said the king, 'it's good to have counsellors who understand mathematics, I suppose; but I would have thought history, philosophy, and language skills might of be more use.'

The professor agreed, 'Maren is strong in all those. Unless you've learned a lot more since I taught you, his language skills are better than yours, and he'd run you a good race in philosophy and history.'

'A gardener in the palace gardens? That doesn't make sense.'

The tutor agreed, but it was a fact.

They discussed the situation for several hours. They concluded that Maren should be paid for a full day's work but would spend half the time in the garden and his afternoons working with Professor Chen. His family was not part of the court, but that did not bar him from being a counsellor. One with a brain as good as Maren's appeared to be would be an asset to the kingdom.

Professor Chen was happy. The princess filled his mornings; she was a bright student, interesting to teach. He felt he was helping to provide her with skills she would need when she became queen. Maren delighted him; each afternoon, the tutor discovered new riches in the young man's mind. He was sure Maren had a secret, but no clues were given.

Dawn often went to the garden in the late afternoon when she knew Maren would be leaving Professor Chen's cottage. Although he was eager to get home at the end of the day, he would stop for a short chat. One day when she was sitting in the pergola, happily breathing in the perfumed air, Durand came striding towards her.

She stood quickly to depart, but he blocked her way and took her hand in his.

'My most dear princess'—his sickly sweet words repelled her—'I have such joy to find you here, making the gardens more beautiful by your presence.'

This was worse than ever. She was desperate to escape.

'Sweet Dawn,' he continued, keeping her hand in his, 'you must be aware of my feelings for you—my great respect and love. We make a perfect pair.'

What was he talking about? She felt ill and weak and so defenceless.

Durand went on and on. She was not listening to the words, just trying to find some means of escape, when she heard 'Then you will become my wife. We were meant for each other.'

'Oh, no, *no*!' She jerked her hand from his grasp and found herself back on the seat behind her.

She looked straight at him and thought she was seeing with her mind rather than her eyes. His face, which had been as pleasant as he could make it, had dropped that mask and had such a look of evil that she felt terrified.

For a moment, he just glared at her and then said clearly and distinctly, 'Beware, my sometime princess. Think well before you deny me. I can destroy you. I will tell your secret to the world unless you agree to marry me.'

What was he talking about?

In the next moment, he told her, 'Perhaps you were fathered by the king but not in wedlock. Bastard-born, you cannot rule.'

'That is a lie.' Her voice was not strong, but she was sure. 'My mother and father were married.'

'No matter. I can start rumours. They grow well in this climate. And I know for a fact that the old king revoked any marriage there might have been. But marry me, my sweet, we'll rule together, and I'll never breathe a word.'

She needed to stand up, leave, but she was too weak. She closed her eyes in her infirmity, perhaps in the faint hope that he would disappear.

The next thing she heard was a squawk. 'Let me go, knave. You'll be for it.'

She opened her eyes to find Maren had caught Durand firmly in an armlock.

When Maren returned from delivering Durand to the guards, he found Dawn still sitting in the pergola. She looked pale.

'Where is he?' she asked.

'Safe with the guards—always several on duty. Let's get you to the cottage. It's closer than the royal apartment.'

Mr Chen gave her a drink of water. The princess closed her eyes and let Maren do the talking. He'd heard all the threats and had at first thought of getting some help but couldn't bear to leave Dawn on her own with the man.

'I heard more than enough to land him in prison,' he concluded.

'Write it all down—every word you remember,' Mr Chen advised and showed Maren paper, ink pot, and a quill pen.

When Maren had finished and the princess was ready, the three of them made their way to the royal apartment.

'The king's with a few of his counsellors,' the queen reported. 'But you, Professor, are one of the few people who could get the guard on duty to open that door. You sound as though you think it's urgent.'

'I do,' the tutor agreed. 'Come on, Maren.'

They had no trouble getting into the council room. Maren felt a bit out of place, much as he had when he was called to his father's council meeting years ago. He was reminded of that day.

He had never actually met the king, but Professor Chen made the introductions, and they were both offered seats at the table.

'Your Majesty,' the tutor began, not calling him Rio as he usually did, 'something has happened which needs to be brought to your attention. Maren was a witness to most of it and rescued the princess, so I wanted—'

The king interrupted, 'The princess. What? Is she all right?'

'Yes, Your Majesty, she is fine and presently with the queen, but I wanted you to hear the story from Maren.'

'Yes.' Rio was impatient. 'Yes. Speak up, young man, what has occurred?'

Maren would have preferred to just let the king read what he had written, but he explained that he was on his way to meet with Professor Chen when he heard voices in the pergola.

'Oh,' remarked His Majesty, 'you're the young fellow he's training up, are you?'

'Yes, Your Majesty, I have that privilege.'

'Well, get on with it. What was happening?' said the king.

'I did not hear the first voice clearly, but then I heard a different voice say no quite loudly. After that, I think it was the voice I had first heard, but it was harsher—threatening. I have written down the words as I remember them.' He handed the paper to the tutor, who passed it to the king. 'I heard the princess denying what he said, but he continued threatening. I caught him from behind with a wrestling hold.'

'Where is he now? Do you know his name?'

Professor Chen answered. 'The guards have him in the small lock-up cell in the palace. His name is . . . Durand Scrope.'

There was silence for a few moments.

The king was reading what Maren had written. When he looked up, his face showed the anger he felt, but he thanked Maren and requested that the professor bring him to the royal apartment at some convenient time in the next few days.

'You were right to interrupt us,' His Majesty said to Professor Chen. 'I appreciate both of you bringing me word straight away.'

The two men went back to check on the princess, were offered a warm drink by the queen, and were not left with much time for their usual discussion.

Maren returned to his present home, rooms behind a healer's establishment, where he lived with Jenny and Jake. As often happened, Jake was too tired to join them, so Maren sat with Jenny and told the story of his day.

'Met king hisself.' She was delighted.

'He's just a man like any other, Jenny.'

She smiled an immense smile. 'But princess's not jus' any woman.'

'What do you mean?' he asked.

'She special to ye.'

'She's the only princess about,' he responded.

'Maren, not to do wi' her be a princess.' She looked at him with wide open eyes.

He turned a bit red. 'No, Jenny, none of your romantics. I'm a gardener.'

Later, when he was trying to go to sleep, he admitted to himself that he was in love with Dawn. He'd have to do something about correcting that. She couldn't be a part of either of his lives. In Riparia, a gardener would not marry a princess. Even if it happened that he ended up fulfilling the old prophecy in the Land of Far, this princess could not go with him; she was required in Riparia.

He wondered once again, as he had so many times, whether anyone would ever come from his former land to take him back.

Chapter 11

Dawn had not seen Maren for more than a week. She had been out visiting or attending functions with Soora on several days, but even when she had waited for him in the pergola, he had not appeared. She did not like to ask Mr Chen directly if his other pupil was away, but maybe she could find out.

'How are Maren's studies going?' she enquired.

'Not well, as a matter of fact,' the tutor responded. 'He's worrying about something, or he's getting sick. I was thinking of suggesting he drop the studying for a bit.'

So Maren was not away. If she had been in contact with Brad, he might have told her that his best gardener was not as good as he had been. Jenny could have added her worries that something was wrong.

The next day, to turn her mind in a different direction, Dawn made a change. Instead of wandering through the bushy and secluded parts of the garden, where she might run into Maren, she walked towards the front of the palace, where there were only a few well-placed bushes and trees with tiny plantings of flowers. Gardeners never spent much time here, but there was space to walk—lawns and gravelled areas where the carriages came and went. She strolled back and forth and then stopped to watch the soldier on duty for a while.

Kahlid's office was close by. Maybe he'd be free to chat. She'd hardly seen him lately, and she needed something to take her mind off Maren. She went into the palace through the door by which she had entered that first time—so long ago. Was she really the same person as that young girl who had stared intently from outside the palace gates?

When she reached the office, the door was open. From the main area, she could see Kahlid standing in his private office with a man who, oddly, reminded her of Maren. They had the same height, the same way of standing, but his clothing was much heavier than was usual—a farmer or perhaps a foreigner.

She heard Kahlid speaking, 'Well, let's go. I'll take you—Oh, Dawn, I didn't know you were there. Let me introduce you to Prince Kim from the Land of Far. I'm just taking him to see your father.' He turned to the other man. 'This is our Princess Dawn.'

When the prince turned towards her, she barely stopped herself from making a loud exclamation. His face was Maren's, and so was his smile.

She managed a polite 'Your Highness', but she felt a bit light-headed. She must be in a terrible state for her mind to impose Maren's features on a stranger. Maybe she could recover some sense of reality by getting acquainted with the prince and seeing him as himself. In any case, she needed something to do.

'I can take him to Father for you,' she offered.

Kahlid shook his head slightly. 'Thank you, Princess, but it's one of my responsibilities.'

'Please, Uncle Kahlid, please.' She was aware that he found it hard to say no to her.

He considered for a moment and then, with a bit of a sigh, said to Kim, 'You're lucky to get the princess as your guide.'

He turned to Dawn. 'Take him straight to the council chambers. His Majesty is probably there. If not, Prince Kim can wait there. A footman will bring him tea or whatever he wishes while you find out where the king is and let him know he has a visitor.'

'Thank you,' she said, delighted with something different and interesting to do.

The regular way was through the corridors, but Dawn led her companion out the first available door. It was a sunny day, and the gardens were worth showing off even if they would not be going through the best part of them. She asked about his country, and he told her of the ten months of snow and the impassable cliff which separated their two countries. 'Although we share that boundary, I had to travel a very long way—through other countries—to get to Riparia.'

She was enjoying Prince Kim's company as they walked on past various entrances to the building.

Quite likely her father would not be in the council chamber. He preferred working in the royal apartment, where he had a small office. The best idea, she thought, would be to go straight to the apartment. In any case, the council chamber was only a short way down the corridor. They might as well go in the easy way by the royal family's private entrance.

They climbed the stairs, and Dawn opened the door into the royal apartment. The queen was speaking to one of the maids.

'Excuse me, Soora,' she said. 'This gentleman is Prince Kim from the Land of Far and wishes to see Father.'

Soora was surprised. Foreign princes were usually expected and were certainly not brought to the royal apartment or by the king's daughter. But Soora recovered quickly. 'Welcome, Prince Kim. I am Queen Soora. If you will wait a moment, I will see if the king can see you now.' She turned to go and then looked back. 'Perhaps you are in need of some refreshment?'

'No. Thank you, Your Majesty. I will wait.'

When a footman had taken the visitor to the king, Soora turned to the princess. 'Come and sit down, Dawn. How did you manage to be the one to bring the prince?'

'I begged Kahlid to let me bring him, Soora. I was bored, and I wanted something different to do.'

Soora sighed. 'Well, I guess no harm is done, but really, Kahlid should have known better. And he should have told you to take the prince to the council chambers.'

'Yes, Soora, and he did tell me. I decided to bring the prince here. I can't truly say I'm sorry, but . . . But I'm sorry I'm not sorry.'

Soora laughed. 'Oh, Dawn, somehow I think your mother would approve of you even when you make up your own mind about things—maybe especially then.'

Meanwhile, the king welcomed the young prince warmly but was disturbed that they had not known beforehand of his coming and made arrangements to celebrate his arrival.

'But we can remedy that,' he said. 'You must stay here in the palace with us, and we will organise a grand dinner, perhaps a ball—'

Prince Kim held up his hand as if to stop him. 'Oh no, Your Majesty. That is most generous of you, but it is best if no one is aware I am here. In fact, I and two other brothers who have also been here at different times have never contacted you at all in order to keep our presence a secret. I am only now having the pleasure of meeting Your Majesty because my eldest brother, King Gareth, felt that I might need your assistance and insisted that I contact you.'

'How can I help?' the king enquired.

'Only if I encounter our enemies here.' The prince began to explain the situation—the original threat to the Land of Far, the major battle, and the skirmishes which followed. 'Now it seems there are still individuals or small groups searching in order to eliminate our youngest brother. Their original threat to our family was the reason we sent him here.'

'What do you mean?' the king asked. 'I do not know of any royal prince living here.'

'No, indeed. It had to be kept secret. Some years ago, we began coming here in order to find him and bring him home. Then it appears that part of the secret became known to our attackers, the Gale Clan, and since then they have been searching in many countries for our brother. We have kept coming to search but sometimes abandoned our own searches here in Riparia in order to pretend to search elsewhere.'

The king was perplexed. 'Where do you think your brother is?'

'After all this time, I guess he could be anywhere,' Kim answered. 'The first time I came, I searched mainly in the western part of Riparia, where the sheer cliff marks the border between our countries. I interviewed many people there. None knew of anyone who had ever come across that border.'

'No,' agreed the king, 'there is no way to cross it.'

Kim smiled. 'It was crossed once, by my brother. That was the area into which we lowered him from the high cliffs.'

The king found it difficult to believe him.

Kim continued, 'I was told of a boy with the same first name as my brother, who had lived there with his parents—or some said his aunt and uncle. It seemed a bare chance that it was my brother—at least a boy of a similar age. None knew where any of that family—Tremain was their name—had gone.'

'You will continue to look for them?' was the king's next question.

'Yes,' said Kim. 'One of my brothers found a Tremain family in the eastern part of your country. There was only a daughter left. She had never met her uncle but thought he had had a boy.'

'Surely you must stay with us while you search,' said the king.

'Your Majesty is most kind, but I will be less obvious if I am just a humble visitor staying in an inn. I am honoured to have met Your Majesty, and I bring you greetings from my eldest brother, King Gareth. Please forget my visit unless I call for your help in an emergency.'

'You must, at least, have a meal with us,' the king insisted, and Kim agreed to that.

Only the royal couple and the princess were at the table with the prince. Dawn was distracted. She tried not to make it obvious that she was staring at Kim. It was foolish to think he looked like Maren. Towards the end of the meal, she excused herself and left the apartment. Once outside, she went straight for the garden cottage. Mr Chen was always her best port in a storm.

She knocked lightly, waited a moment, and was about to open the door when it swung back. Maren had opened it.

He was the same height as Kim. His eyes were the same colour, his nose the same shape.

'You are alike.' She was so startled she spoke out loud.

'What?' Maren stared back at her. 'Alike? Who?'

'Prince Kim,' she answered.

Maren grabbed her hand. 'Who? Where?'

'Prince Kim in the royal apartment,' she said. 'He came this afternoon.'

'Show me.' It was more a command than a request. He was pulling her back the way she had come. She wasn't sure if he even realised he had grasped her hand so firmly.

They ran through the garden, up the royals' private stairs. Maren barged into the door of the apartment, and it banged open.

For more than a moment, no one moved or spoke. Then Kim sprang from his chair at the table, and Maren flew towards him. They locked together.

The king, queen, and princess stared, but no one spoke.

Kim recovered first. He held Maren firmly with one arm but turned towards the others. 'Your Majesties,' he said, 'this is my brother, Prince Maren of Far.'

Then he turned slowly back and looked at his younger brother. 'Where have you been all this time?'

'No,' Maren replied. 'Where have you been? I thought you had forgotten me altogether.'

'We never forgot. This is our fourth trip here to look for you. Lance and Ivan—each came once, and this is my second try. The first time when the fighting seemed to have stopped and we thought it was finished, I searched for you, mainly in the area near the sheer cliffs. I spoke to person after person. The only lead was a family named Tremain.'

'That was a good lead,' Maren said.

'Except no one knew where they'd gone, and most said the boy was named Maren but was their son or nephew.'

Maren reminded him, 'I was supposed to blend in'. Then he remembered there were others in the room. He held on to Kim but spoke to the royal couple. 'Your Majesties, I do apologise. We've been talking as though no one else was present. Please forgive us.'

'But, of course,' the queen assured him. 'Is this your brother, Prince Kim, the one you came to find?'

'Yes, Your Majesty,' Kim answered. But he was in shock, finding it almost impossible to speak.

They stared at each other in wonder until the king broke the silence. 'The story of your country is one we don't know well. You will have to enlighten us. Who were the attacking forces?'

Kim straightened up and gave a short history of the Gale Clan and told of their threat to assassinate the whole royal family.

'Did you all survive?' the queen asked.

'No, Your Majesty, not all,' Kim replied. 'Our father and Harold, the second eldest, were killed in the first major attack. Our fourth brother, Jarrah, died in a later skirmish. The country generally was crushed, the people ready to give up the struggle.'

The king spoke, 'Your eldest brother then has been king for some time, I think.'

'He's the one who saved the country,' Kim said. 'He never wished to be king, but no one could have done a better job. His spirit and strength have energised us all. I hope Your Majesty may meet him someday.'

'It would be a great pleasure,' Rio answered.

'You should go to Far to join us in the celebrations when I bring Maren back,' Kim told them. 'There will be bonfires, new songs written for the occasion, even dancing in the snow.'

'When will that be?' asked the queen.

'Soon, very soon,' Kim replied. 'We must return speedily and let everyone rejoice. It will make the people feel as though spring has come even in the midst of winter.'

Most of the people in the room were smiling. But Dawn was not. Was Maren going to disappear altogether? She looked towards him and found that he was staring straight at her. He was not smiling either.

Now that Kim had found his brother, the king and queen were eager for the two princes to stay at the palace. Kim agreed gladly, and the king sent a footman to bring his bags from the inn. Maren, however, turned down the offer. 'It is most kind of Your Majesties, but I must return to my parents—my foster parents, of course. They will be expecting me.'

'No,' Kim countered, 'you must stay with me. I cannot let you go now I have found you and certainly not on your own into the city.'

Maren laughed. 'I've been going back and forth—palace to city, city to palace—for years. What's the problem?'

'Someone from the Gale Clan could still be searching for you,' Kim said. 'Although the last sizeable band murdered their own leader and melted back into wherever they came from, they may still have spies in Riparia.'

'Oh, Kim, even if they still do, they don't know you've found me.' Maren was adamant. 'I have to go home. There's no way I'm going to just forget about Jenny and Jake.'

The king turned to Kim. 'Would you like me to send a guard with him?'

Maren was the first to answer. 'No, no, thank you, Your Majesty. That would make me stand out. I'd be in danger then.'

'Well, this will have to be your last night with these people,' Kim declared. 'I guess you do need to say goodbye to them.'

Maren just stood in silence and stared at his brother before he spoke. 'Jenny and Jake are not just "these people". They took me in when I had no home. They cared for me as if I was their own son. I won't be saying goodbye to them in a hurry.'

Everyone was looking at him. The atmosphere in the room had turned sombre. Kim looked confused and angry.

Then Maren made another statement. He didn't want to spoil the reunion, but Kim needed to understand the situation. 'I don't know how soon you're thinking of going back to Far, big brother, but I will not be leaving here until Jake and Jenny are well set up for the future.'

It seemed the wrong moment to leave although he was long overdue and Jenny would be worrying. He was also struggling to find a way to speak with Dawn even though he didn't know what to say to her. He was a prince; to love a princess was now quite reasonable. But if he was not to stay in Riparia . . .

Dawn herself solved the first problem. 'It'll be quicker for you, Maren, to go by the main gate. I'll come with you to see that the guard lets you out there. I need a bit of a walk.'

They left together and went down the stairs without speaking. Once outside, Dawn asked, 'Are you going back to Far to live?'

Maren looked so sad she almost wished she hadn't asked, but she had to know. They walked a short way before Maren answered, 'It seems that's what Kim came for, Your Highness.'

'Your Highness! Maren, you've never called me that before. You were the only gardener who never did.'

'Now,' he said, sounding bitter, 'you can call me Your Highness as well.'

She had never heard him speak so harshly. 'Yes,' she said the word slowly and softly over the lump in her throat. She spoke to the guard, wished Maren goodnight, and returned to the palace, sure she had lost Maren whatever happened.

Chapter 12

It was much later than usual when Maren, annoyed with himself for speaking rudely to Dawn, got back to his home. Jenny was concerned.

'I am so sorry, Jenny. Time just lost all meaning.' He told her his brother had turned up. He even told her something of his story. When he admitted to being born a prince, she said, 'You always were a prince to me.' And he gave her a kiss.

But then she said, 'Now y're a proper prince, ye ken have princess.'

Maren walked outside into the tiny yard and looked up to see that there would be no stars tonight. Grey clouds filled the sky. *Appropriate*, he thought.

Later, when he went to bed, sleep was hard to find. His words to the princess haunted him.

His dreams were troubled with his father and Princess Dawn arguing about who owned a faded green royal gardener's uniform.

The next morning, Maren reported at the usual time to Brad's office. Instead of getting a job assignment, he was told the king required him to go to the royal apartment.

His steps were slow, but his mind was busy working out what to say to the princess if he had an opportunity. He must apologise. He was relieved to find her alone.

'Princess Dawn,' he began. She turned to him and for a brief moment, he forgot what he had come to say. She was so beautiful. He jerked his mind back to the apology. 'I'm ashamed of the way I spoke to you last night. I am so sorry. It was inexcusable.'

'Maren,' she said, 'you were upset.'

'But not with you. Can you forgive me?' he asked.

She answered steadily although she felt far from steady, 'I do, of course. I will miss you when you go.'

When he didn't know what to say to that, she changed the subject. 'Could you tell me the prophecy about the seventh son? Do you know it all?'

'I think it was the first thing we all learned,' he told her. 'After six sons, a seventh one. The winds foretell where he shall sit upon the throne, all will be well. That's it.'

'But, Maren,' Dawn said, 'that doesn't mention the Land of Far.'

'True,' he admitted, 'but that's where the prophecy's been spoken long before it was written down.'

'Will you become king as soon as you get there?'

'Oh, no.' He laughed joylessly. 'Probably never. My eldest brother is king. Then there are three more elder brothers. Kim tells me the king has two sons, and the other brothers have one son each. There are also four young princesses. I don't know what I can do to really be of use.'

Dawn looked bewildered. 'I don't understand.' After a moment, a sudden smile lit her face. 'Why, Maren, in order to fulfil the prophecy, you'll have to do it in another country—not Far.'

He had never heard of the prophecy being interpreted that way.

He wanted to go on with the discussion, but just then Kim dashed in. 'At last, little brother. But why are you wearing that uniform again?'

'Aside from being what I always wear to work, it's the best-looking outfit I own,' Maren said.

'What? You don't mean that.' Kim looked annoyed.

'I've no money for fancy clothes nor occasions to wear them,' Maren explained.

'Ah, well,' Kim said, 'we'll have to remedy that. Settled arrangements with your foster parents, did you? So we can leave without delay?'

That silenced Maren for at least a full minute. 'No. It can't be settled just like that. I don't know where to find a place for them, and I haven't told them yet that I'm leaving. It's a big—'

Kim interrupted. 'You haven't told them? You went to do that last night.'

'Kim, stop. You're not listening,' Maren accused. He repeated much of what he'd said the night before and agreed to start working for a solution. 'Though I've only got one maybe possible idea where to begin.'

The brothers were still at odds when Dawn left the apartment and headed for Kahlid's office.

Kim thought decent clothes were something to be attended to. When Rio heard about it, he offered two suits to be made by the royal tailor, and it was arranged that Maren could be measured a bit later in the morning.

The older brother sent Maren off—without worrying about the Gale Clan. 'Check on your one idea and be back here promptly.'

Maren returned to the building where he lived but not to Jenny and Jake. He went to the front to speak to the owner. He was a healer who looked like a wizard with his long white hair and beard. He agreed that Maren's parents could stay; he might be able to reduce the rent but not by much. The healer had always helped them with potions and pills without charge and was happy to continue that, but he didn't know of anywhere they could live without regular payment.

Maren knew they had an amount from the sale of their house, but it was getting smaller every month; his pay covered little more than the rent. How could they manage? And how could he support them from the Land of Far? He knew there was no extra money that he would find in the snow country, where no one was rich, not even the royal family.

Kim went with Maren down corridors and around corners to the tailor's premises. Maren was measured and chose materials.

'Two days, and they'll be ready,' the tailor promised.

As they were leaving, he called them back and handed Maren a parcel. 'It's a suit I made for my boy—almost exactly your size. I can make him another. This'll come in handy for you perhaps.'

Maren was exuberant in his thanks.

The newly found prince had done a lot of thinking although involved in various activities during the morning. They were nearly back to the apartment, walking through the royal corridor, when he pushed Kim into the library. It was not used much, and there was no one else there.

'Hey, what?' Kim objected as he staggered a bit but stayed upright.

'We need to have a talk,' Maren said, pulling two chairs together and sitting on one of them.

Kim sat too. 'What about, little brother? Most things are going fine except for your so-called parents.'

'That's your opinion' was the reply. 'I'm not so sure about this whole thing, and as it's my life, I've decided to be part of the decisions.'

'You are, aren't you? What are you saying?' Kim was confused. 'It's all about you.'

'About me but decided by you,' Maren said. 'I'm going to make the decision about whether I go back to Far or stay here.'

'What? Are you crazy? Of course, you go back. The country needs to have their seventh son visible, working with them, giving them hope.' Kim was adamant.

Maren wasn't convinced. 'I don't see that my going back will have much of an impact—maybe for a day or a week but nothing more.

Kim put forward his side of the argument, and Maren kept countering it. He pointed out the fact that it was almost impossible for him to ever become a Far king. Then he got to the main issue. 'Big brother, I'll make you a promise. If Princess Dawn agrees to marry me, and the king gives his permission, I'll be staying in Riparia. If not, I'll go to Far with you.'

Kim looked pale and distraught. For a moment, his body tilted sideways. He put his hands over his eyes and bent forward. When he opened his eyes, he had difficulty getting out what he wanted to say. 'You . . . you can't—I found you.'

Maren sat still and said nothing.

Kim couldn't believe what he'd heard. 'You don't mean it. This isn't . . . it isn't happening.'

It was hard on Kim. The younger brother hoped he was not causing an irreparable break in their relationship. He was aware that there was every possibility he would still end up in the country where he had been born. In all probability, to the princess, he was just a gardener. But he would at least have tried following his heart.

* * *

Meanwhile, Dawn had taken Maren's problem of arrangements for Jake and Jenny to Kahlid. He had accommodated Mia; perhaps he could help. Indeed, he thought there would be a place for them in his diversified household, which worked more as a community of people than was usual in other wealthy establishments.

On her way back to the apartment, Dawn felt despondent. In trying to help Maren, she had probably hastened his departure. In any case, she had no proof that he considered there was a relationship between them. Recently, he'd kept out of her way quite successfully. Even if he stayed in Riparia as a prince, there was no reason to think . . .

She felt tears coming and scolded herself. Her mother had been courageous and lived her life as it had to be. She had better pull herself together.

She found Soora and suggested they go to see Mia. Both Soora and Mia were practical and supportive. They would do her good; they would help her dispel the cold despair she was feeling. She wrote a note to Maren before she and Soora walked to the Aman residence with their usual escort.

* * *

Sometime later, both Far princes quietly re-entered the royal apartment. Maren was hoping to speak to the princess and, at the same time, intimidated by the thought that speaking to her could put an end to all his hopes.

The king was the only person in sight. 'The ladies went to Kahlid's to see Mia—only expecting to stay briefly, back any time now,' he told them. 'Oh, Maren, Dawn left you a note.' He handed it over and went off to the council chambers.

The note read, 'Maren, have a chat with Kahlid. He thinks he may be able to give your parents a home.' She had not even signed it, but that was only because she could not decide how to do so.

When Kim saw it, he was encouraged. The princess would surely not be bothered helping to find a place for Jenny and Jake if she wanted Maren to stay in Riparia. Maren thought the same, but they did not share their thoughts.

Maybe his standing up for what he wanted and upsetting Kim was just a pointless exercise, but Maren was determined to go through with it, whatever the outcome. He decided to try to catch the princess on her way back from Kahlid's, before she went into the palace. Kim went to his room and Maren went back to the garden.

There was a bench from which he could observe the gate. He watched the comings and goings on the road outside and saw one person let in by the guard.

Then he saw the uniformed footman and got up to meet the ladies. But there was only one with him—Soora. 'Dawn stayed at Kahlid's,' she told him. 'Kara was there with a few of her friends.'

He knew it wasn't the end of the world, but Maren felt as if it was.

'Are you coming in, Maren?' the queen asked.

'No, thank you, Your Majesty. I think not,' he replied, his voice full of sadness.

Soora thought he looked as miserable as Dawn did. Was he unhappy to be found by his brother? She had thought it was a joy to both of them.

However, the queen was sensitive to emotions of others and thought she knew the cause of both Dawn's and Maren's unhappiness.

She had a notion. 'Maren, I wonder if you could do something for me this evening.'

'Of course, Your Majesty. How can I help you?'

'I've promised to send a carriage for the princess. The group is going to an entertainment just outside the city, and she wanted to come back before the others who plan to stay quite late. I was going to go myself to keep her company, but I would be grateful if you could manage to go in my place to bring her back to the palace.'

She thought she was on the right track when she saw Maren's face. He seemed to stand up taller than before when he said, 'I am at your service, Your Majesty. I shall be ready whenever you wish.'

'Thank you, Prince Maren. Please come and have lunch with us. It will be served in about half an hour, and we can discuss details.'

When he agreed, they walked together towards the entry to the palace.

Although the day seemed to go slowly, Maren had something to look forward to which made him both nervous and excited. He had lunch with his brother and the royal couple. The queen informed him where and when the carriage would pick him up; she again expressed gratitude for his assistance. He was glad to have the tailor's gift as a change from his gardener's uniform.

It was a closed carriage, smaller than the one Dawn had ridden in to Riverwood. It was drawn by only one horse and had one coachman.

It was a wonder to Maren, who had never ridden in a carriage. In his childhood, he had once or twice been in an open sleigh, but the Land of Far was not a place for carriages.

On the way, he lost nearly all his hope. He changed what he planned to say to Dawn over and over, but he was afraid none of it would do. There seemed to be no way to go. Perhaps it would be best to just try to appreciate having this last time with Princess Dawn. If he asked and she refused, both of them would be uncomfortable. Before he had come to a definite decision, the carriage had reached its destination.

The archway where the carriage stopped was brightly lit. A series of wall sconces held more candles than Maren could conveniently count. It was a brilliant display. He stepped down on to the ground and walked through the arch towards the grand building behind it. An official in a splendid cloak with elaborate decorations across his chest stopped him.

As he was representing the queen, Maren gave his name as Prince Maren of Far but felt he was talking about someone else. He said he had come to take Princess Dawn back to the palace.

'I will send for her.' The official summoned a footman to inform her.

Maren did not have long to wait. She came hurrying towards him. 'Why, Maren, it's you. How nice of you to take the time when you're so busy.' *Perhaps he had come on purpose to say goodbye.*

'The queen asked me to take her place,' he explained.

'Oh.' Dawn was beside him, but his feet seemed glued to the ground. 'Shall we go?' she suggested. 'It looks like the carriage is here.'

It was, but the coachman was not in sight. Maren helped the princess up into the carriage and joined her.

'I'm really glad to see you,' she said as they seated themselves. 'At one stage, I wondered if you'd gone away. I'd seen so little of you.' That wasn't what she would have liked to have said. She was nervous and went on disastrously, 'Now you'll be about to say goodbye and head off to your own country.'

Maren felt terrible. He certainly couldn't ask her to marry him; she was quite ready to see him off. 'Dawn—Princess Dawn,' he was babbling, 'I don't want . . . I can't go to Far without—I . . . it's hard for me . . . If you only knew.' He was silent and hardly dared to look up at the princess.

She wanted to comfort him; he seemed so distressed. 'Tell me what I need to know, what I don't understand.'

'I might not have to leave,' he said very softly.

She smiled. 'You'll stay in Riparia? You won't have to go to Far?'

'No,' he said, 'at least not if you'll marry me.'

What had he done? That wasn't how he meant to say it. She'd push him out of the carriage.

But the princess was glowing. From the light of the candles in the wall sconces, he could see that her smile was as wide as it could be.

'Of course, I'll marry you.' Her voice was as happy as he'd ever heard it. 'But you didn't have to wait until I knew you were a prince to ask me.'

The coachman had come back. He knocked on the carriage door and apologised for keeping them waiting. 'Didn't think ye be so speedy, Your Highness.'

'It's fine, Ahan,' she assured him.

They were on their way, and it was hard to talk as they rattled over the rough roads. But they'd had enough words for the moment. They were both in shock. Although it was exactly what they wanted, it was a complete reversal of their dismal expectations. The best they could do was to hold hands and look at each other.

Shortly before they reached the palace gates, Dawn knocked on the front panel of the carriage. When it stopped, the coachman came to the door. 'Let us out just inside the gates, Ahan,' the princess said. 'It's a nice evening, and we've been sitting too long.'

'Just so, Your Highness.'

When they got out, they stood and watched the carriage disappear. Hand in hand, they began walking. They were strangely shy with each other, as though there was some further ritual to go through before they could express the strong emotions they felt.

Maren was the first to speak. 'When I was just a member of the garden staff, would you actually have considered marrying me?'

'I did.' Dawn was remembering. 'I wondered what my father would say. But how could he object?'

'Because of your mother?' Maren asked.

Dawn agreed. But then, as they neared the entry to the palace, she felt she needed to confirm the reality of what had happened between them, which only an hour ago had seemed a complete impossibility.

She stopped and turned towards Maren. She felt she was swinging between wild joy and uncertainty. 'Will it really happen, Maren? Really? When? Will we truly marry?'

'I think I need to do the right thing and speak to your father first.' Maren was trying to keep from totally exploding with joyful laughter or kissing Dawn with enough strength to frighten her. 'Tomorrow wouldn't be too soon for me.'

'You'll come tomorrow to see Father?' she asked.

'Tomorrow,' he said.

'You'll be early?'

'I may be able to wait till the sun rises, but I promise to be early.'

She laughed. 'You couldn't come too soon.'

They clasped hands tightly for a moment, and she vanished into the palace.

She had never felt so happy, but she didn't want to share it till tomorrow. She wanted to be alone. She was pleased that her father and Soora were speaking with several of the councillors. They gave her a wave, and she retreated happily to her room. She wasn't sure she would be able to sleep, but she was warm and happy, and her dreams were beautiful.

When she woke in the morning, it was very early. There was little light. She dressed quickly, left the apartment, and stepped into the garden. It was full of mystery and promise. She stayed near the door, but Maren did not appear. Dawn's euphoria was leaking away when a gardener began pruning nearby. She went inside, climbing wearily up the stairs to a breakfast she didn't want. Was last night just a dream?

After breakfast, there was still no Maren. Had something terrible happened to him? After a bit, she wrote a note to him and had a footman take it to Jenny's house, where he had planned to spend the night.

Jenny had not worried when Maren did not return. She thought he must have stayed at the palace. Now Jenny was worried as well.

Soora and the king were there when the footman reported back.

'What is it?' the queen asked when she saw Dawn's pale, anxious face.

Kim was consulted but had no idea where his brother might be. So the palace guard was informed, and two contingents were sent out to search the city.

Chapter 13

Maren himself had no idea where he was. On his way back to Jenny's, he had been knocked down by two men who gagged, blindfolded, and bound him in ropes. After they cleared his pockets, they deposited him roughly on to what seemed to be a sort of handcart, and he was given a rough ride during which he thought he must have passed out a couple of times. His body was bruised all over, and his head was aching badly. They dragged him off the cart and propelled him into a building. It seemed they went through a couple of doorways before they deposited him on a mattress and threw a blanket over him.

They removed his gag and blindfold but didn't speak to him except to growl, 'Keep y'r mouth shut 'er we'll do it for ye,' when he tried to discover their motivation for kidnapping him.

The ropes were not expertly tied, and he managed to loosen them. But he stayed under the blanket. When they checked on him, which they did a few times, they were not aware that he was no longer secured.

The third time they went in, he asked quietly, 'Food? Water?'

'Tomorrow,' one of them said. The other just laughed and told him, 'Yer majestic ken sleep now.'

They had a quick look at him soon after that. Then he heard glasses clinking and celebratory shouting, after which there was singing—loud, aggressive—followed by short silences and then a long one.

Maren had completely untangled the ropes; he climbed off the mattress and stood up. He felt unsteady, but he was upright. The room was tiny. Beside the mattress was a small chest, but there was no other furniture. Some light came through the window on the opposite side of the room to the door.

When he examined the window, he found it was also a door—quite flimsy. He inspected it with his fingertips and began gently encouraging it to move. He got it open, not quite soundlessly. He stepped out of the room and pulled the door slowly until it shut. He breathed deeply as he looked around. There was no sound of movement behind him.

It was a small yard, empty of anything of value. He picked his way across piles of junk and walked through a gateless opening on to a rough, rutted track. Light came from across the alley. It was obviously a market area; perhaps soon people would begin to arrive to set up shops.

Maren moved away quickly. He had no idea where he was or which direction would be best to take. Soon he had left his captors far behind, but he had also passed into a farming area outside the city where it would be harder to find anything he recognised.

The sun had come up, and the road was clear ahead of him. It was a pleasant area, but he was slowing down—tired, thirsty, and hungry. His head was throbbing. Once he collapsed; when he came to, he was lying at the edge of the road. He forced himself to stand and walked on. He was anxious about what Dawn would be thinking. A farmer in a cart started to slow down but speeded up and moved quickly away when he got close enough to see him clearly. Maren looked down at himself. He was a mess. The new suit the tailor had given him was torn, filthy, and wrinkled. Never, even as a gardener, had he been so dishevelled-looking. He couldn't see his face, but if it looked like the rest of him . . .

Maren passed an old neglected orchard. He managed to climb across some fallen wires and found a few apples. He munched on them as he walked.

From a small rise, he saw the city and changed direction. He walked across paddocks, struggled over fences, and forded a stream. At the stream, he sloshed water on his face and tried to make himself look a bit more presentable. It was not successful. As he came into a busy road, he saw three palace guards watching the people going by. He headed for them. They could certainly tell him how to get to the palace, maybe help him get there or clean up a bit.

'Excuse me, gentlemen,' he addressed the guardsmen, 'I need some help.'

They turned to him. He did not understand their reaction. Two looked at him in silence, with a smile gradually spreading across their faces. But the third one—much the youngest—almost bounced up and down in his glee.

'We've found you!' he shouted. 'We've found you. You're the Far prince, aren't you?'

'Yes,' he said, feeling only pain, exhaustion, and confusion.

The guards wanted information about his captors. They took note of Maren's description of the two men and his suggestion that the location where he had been held was close to a market.

After that, everything seemed to combine to whirl him towards the palace. The guardsmen commandeered a carriage with its driver, who did not look pleased to be asked to carry the unsavoury character accompanied by the young guardsman.

It was a short trip. The excited guardsman, whose name was Frit, helped Maren out of the carriage and paid the driver. He spoke to a footman who had approached, and they went directly to the royal apartment.

Unkempt and collapsing—only held up by adrenalin and Frit's arm—Maren was suddenly face to face with Dawn. In fact, a moment later, he found himself encircled by her arms. Something more than adrenalin took hold, and they had their first passionate kiss—or at least the beginning of one—surrounded by an astonished company.

The maid and footmen in attendance were agog. Soora quickly realised who he was; she was delighted for Dawn, while the king looked on in total amazement. Kim felt a failure; he had found Maren, but now he would not be bringing him back to his people in the Land of Far.

The kiss only lasted momentarily. Almost the moment it began, Dawn felt Maren collapsing in her arms. Frit, who was beside him, caught him before he hit the ground. Quickly they got his grimy and battered body on to a beautifully upholstered royal couch. Dawn stood looking down at him. Was he still breathing?

Kim forgot his disappointment and, with great concern for his brother, felt for Maren's still-beating pulse.

'Nothing to worry about, Your Highness,' Frit assured Dawn. 'Total exhaustion's all that's wrong with him.'

'You know that for sure, do you, guardsman?' the king asked.

'Yes, Your Majesty,' Frit responded. 'From what he told us, he'd no sleep since night before last; was taken by some thugs on his way home; beaten, bound, gagged, and blindfolded; and's been walking without knowing where he was going since before daybreak.'

But Kim, who had some knowledge of simple medicine, disagreed. 'He's unconscious—not responding to stimulus as he would if only asleep.'

Two footmen carried Maren to a bed. He was covered with a blanket and watched over by the royal family.

Kim, who would have preferred to stay beside his brother, had been called upon to assist in interviewing two men apprehended in a muddled and staggering condition. They fit Maren's description but seemed to have trouble communicating in the Riparian language. It was thought that Kim might be better able to question them. He did establish that they had been loosely connected with a section of the Gale Clan and had hoped to get well rewarded for capturing the seventh son. They appeared to be unaware of how to contact anyone who might reward them; they did not know of the break-up of the main section of the clan.

However, Kim was the one sitting near the bed in the late afternoon when Maren began groaning and then flinging his arms about. He opened his eyes, and then feeling all the stiffness and bruising with every move, he was still. His eyes studied the room.

Kim stood by the bed. 'Welcome back, little brother. I'm glad you made it.'

'What?' He looked at his brother. 'Kim, where am I?'

Kim smiled. 'In my bed at the palace—Riparia, of course.'

Maren lay there, thinking. He asked, 'How did I get here? Last thing I remember was—' he paused—'walking and walking forever, then talking to some guardsmen. Or perhaps they were part of the dream.'

'No,' Kim said. 'They were real. What was the dream?'

'Riding in a carriage into the palace precinct, going right into the royal apartment, and . . .' He smiled. 'It was a good dream.'

'Yes,' Kim agreed, 'especially when you kissed the princess.'

'How did you know that?' Maren was astonished.

'It wasn't a dream,' Kim said. 'You kissed her right in front of us all. But it was the shortest kiss on record.'

'It really happened?' To Maren, it didn't seem possible.

'You better not try it again. It's obviously dangerous for you. Two seconds, and you collapsed,' Kim teased. He went on, 'I promised to notify everyone when you woke. The king wants to speak to you. The queen wants to send in food and offers you a bath.'

Maren asked, 'You'll do the honours with the water?'

'Wake up, Maren,' Kim countered. 'You're a prince in Riparia now. This isn't Far, where the royal family's just part of the community. Here, there are footmen to carry the hot water.'

The footmen filled the bath and added healing salts to the water. Maren's grazes stung, but it felt wonderful to soak in a hot bath and let his bruised body relax and begin to mend. His head hurt, but his main thoughts were of Dawn. Had she looked in on him as he slept? Where was she now?

Clean, clothed in top and trousers borrowed from Kim, Maren enjoyed a bowl of soup the queen had insisted he ate before seeing the king. When he asked about the princess, he was told that Dawn had been ordered not to speak with him until after he met with her father.

It was with both curiosity and some trepidation that he went to Rio's small office in the apartment.

'Welcome, Prince Maren.' The king's greeting sounded friendly.

Maren replied, 'Thank you, Your Majesty. I am grateful for your hospitality and that of the queen.'

'It is our pleasure. I hope we may have the pleasure frequently in the future.' He motioned to a chair. 'Please sit down.'

Maren sat and wondered what was coming.

'My daughter tells me', the king said, 'that you were planning to come to see me first thing this morning. I realise you could not help that plan being disrupted, but is there something you wish to discuss with me?'

'Yes, indeed, Your Majesty.' Maren did not hesitate. 'I wish to ask for your daughter's hand in marriage.

The king smiled. 'I had an idea it was something along those lines, and I hope I can respond in a manner both you and Dawn desire. I have always promised myself to let my daughter make her own choice in the matter. However'—he paused and looked serious—'in this particular case, there are perhaps more consequences to be considered than the usual.'

Maren was not sure what to say and kept quiet.

'You know, of course,' the king continued, 'that my daughter is the only real and viable heir to the throne of Riparia.'

'Yes, Your Majesty,' Maren agreed.

'I have heard your brother Prince Kim speak about your returning to the Land of Far. If you did so and remained there permanently, the situation would not be workable. Much as it would nearly break my heart to deny my daughter in this case, I do not think I would have an option.'

Maren had held himself back from interrupting the king, but now he spoke with great force, 'No, Your Majesty. I have told my brother—I told him that I would stay in your country if the princess agreed to marry me and you gave your permission. I realise that the princess must stay here. If you do not give permission, I will return to Far.'

The king's smile was broader than before. 'Prince Maren, I cannot tell you how delighted I am. Were I to pick a husband for my daughter, I do not imagine I could find a better candidate. Professor Chen has given such glowing accounts of you that I am sure I can agree to the marriage with all my heart.'

Maren felt as if joy had knocked all the breath out of him.

'The princess and the queen await us,' the king said. 'Shall we go and tell them the good news?'

However, when they moved out of the office, the king's face grew serious, and his announcement when they reached the two ladies was as official sounding as he could make it. 'Following the tradition of the royal family of Riparia, I wish to announce that I have chosen a husband for the heir to the throne. Princess Dawn, I present to you Prince Maren of Far, whom you are commanded to marry in due course.'

Maren decided to play along with the king. He moved forward and most ceremoniously but, with sparkling eyes, lifted Dawn's right hand to his lips. 'I am charmed by your beauty, Your Highness. Will you join me on a walk in the garden so that we may become better acquainted?'

Dawn was both laughing and crying as they left the apartment and went out into the garden.

Maren was now happy to stay in the palace, but before the day came to an end, both he and Dawn were clear that Jenny and Jake must be told of the developments.

Dawn had earlier sent a footman with the news that Maren had been found. This time, they both went by carriage, causing a stir in the backstreet where Maren had lived with his foster parents.

Although Jenny and Jake were generally unruffled by many things which excited or agitated others, Maren's arrival—looking so vibrant and joyful—with the only princess Riparia possessed was breathtaking, and both of them were thrilled.

Jake said, 'Proud of you, son. Worked your way every step.'

Jenny was speechless for once. She finally managed 'I love ye both' and cried when the two of them kissed her and gave her a hug.

Maren insisted that he bring the tea. 'I know where your best brew is.' He wanted Jenny to get acquainted with Dawn. The two women bonded almost immediately. They were chatting like old friends as Maren helped Jake to a seat in the kitchen.

Both wanted to know about the other, but Dawn got Jenny talking first. 'Eldest girl in fam'ly of eight, I was, with a brother older. Life not easy. Married late 'cause was carin' for me brothers 'n' sisters. Jake 'n' me, we was wantin' babes, 'n' none there be. Then the joy of it for twelve years. Him 'n' Jake, the three of us . . .' Jenny paused and wiped her eyes.

'So you had a son?' the princess asked.

'Name Samuel,' the older woman said. 'God took from me afore he turned thirteen.'

They were silent. Dawn reached over and held both Jenny's hands in hers.

The older woman explained how Maren had come into their home and filled the empty space. 'A true son to us,' she said.

Before the princess left, she hugged Jenny and said, 'There's a place for you at the palace. I'm going to find just the spot where you and Jake'll be happy, where you can grow your herbs and make your lovely teas. I feel like I've found the grandmother I've always wanted, and I need you close by.'

'Dear chile,' Jenny remonstrated, quite unaware of addressing Dawn in an unusual way, 'couldn't live in palace—not us two.'

'Don't say no till I show you what I find,' the princess said. 'We'll be back soon.'

* * *

The next three months were full of wonder and delight for Maren and Dawn, but they also held difficulties and learning experiences.

Maren slipped back easily into his role as a prince, strengthened and better informed by his years as a gardener. However, fitting back into a situation where a royal father was in charge could be painful. Rio was friendly and eager to get along well with his soon-to-be son-in-law, but he had been ruling in his own way for too long to accept new ideas easily.

The king made Maren a member of his council, but when the new member proposed that the future queen should also be on the council, Rio originally refused. However, after a week or so, he recognised the wisdom of the prince's suggestion, and Dawn became the first female member.

The princess had always tried to forget the role that loomed in her future, but with Maren's help, she was learning to move comfortably into experiences which helped to prepare her for what lay ahead.

For a while, she was preoccupied with finding an acceptable home for Jake and Jenny. She knew they did not wish to live in the palace itself, but she thought there must be somewhere in the spacious gardens which surrounded it that would suit them well. Maren remembered a small stone building at the back of the palace, surrounded by equipment sheds and Brad's office.

'I don't think I ever saw inside it, but it looked as if it had been built as a home,' he said.

When Dawn went to have a look, Brad was dismissive. 'Head gardener lived there years ago—not fit for much now, except to store old tools . . . dilapidated, ready to fall down or be demolished.'

'Oh, no,' the princess remonstrated. 'It's well built and could be fixed up. We'll put a neat little fence round it—space for herbs and a seat.'

'Can't have folks living there,' Brad insisted. 'Get in the way.'

But it's hard to win an argument with the heir to the throne. After Jenny and Jake moved in, the head gardener and his staff were frequent visitors, sampling freshly baked muffins or biscuits and cups of herbal tea.

The princess was often at Stone Cottage, as they called it. Her 'grandmother' added something special to the support she had always felt from Mia and Soora.

As the weeks passed, the royal dressmaker began work on the wedding gown. Dawn took Jenny with her to one of the fittings. The older woman was overawed by the intricate embroidery on the gown and the gown itself, but she was even more amazed when the princess insisted on having her 'grandmother' measured and ordered a simple but elegant gown for her. When it was finished and brought to Stone Cottage, Jenny was afraid she would never dare to put it on.

However, when the wedding day came, she slipped it on with great care and felt as though she was a queen herself when she looked in the mirror.

At the ceremony, she sat with Jake under the high vaulted ceiling of the great church in the centre of Aviol. They were placed in the midst of Maren's family. Kim had managed to convince King Gareth and his three other brothers, plus all their wives and children, to make the long trip from the Land of Far to attend the wedding and reconnect with their lost brother.

The immense space was full with the group from Far, dignitaries and important people from all areas of Riparia, palace servants and gardeners, and the members of the general populace who had managed to find an empty spot.

But there were still people outside—so many of them. When the prince and princess went out into the sunshine as man and wife, the explosion of rejoicing from the crowd dismayed Dawn.

Maren reassured her, 'It's louder, and there are more people than ever gathered in Far. But they're just expressing their love. Even as a small child, I had to learn not to be afraid of them and to wave and smile.' Maren helped her up into the sparkling royal carriage. Both of them gave genuine smiles and happy waves as they drove to the palace.

Once they reached the grand ballroom and magnificent dining hall area, a cluster of small princesses and princes, Maren's nieces and nephews, gathered around them. In the few days the Far families had been in Riparia, the children had decided that Maren and Dawn belonged to them in a special way. Part of the charm was certainly Maren's stories. Some of them came from his own experiences, and some, he told them, were from his grandmother, who had been a wind-listener.

'Today we're all part of the story,' Maren said, smiling at all nine of them. 'This is a story the wind will be telling for years to come. Keep your eyes and ears open, and some day, you'll be able to tell this story to your children even if you can't hear other stories from the wind.'

'I've heard the wind lots, and it's never told me any stories,' complained Gareth's older boy.

Mita, Lance's daughter, who told everyone she was 'five, going on six', was jumping up and down. 'It's told me, Uncle Maren, lots of times.' She was smiling right down to her toes, which couldn't seem to stop dancing.

'Can you tell us how to listen, Mita? Can you tell us what you do?' Maren was intrigued. He had thought that the skill may have died out perhaps a couple of generations ago.

'I go outside and sit down by the big rock or an old tree,' she said.

'And then?' Maren prompted.

'I just keep quiet. I don't make a sound, and I sit very still until every bit of me is quiet—inside and out.' The little girl looked up at Maren, her eyes big and serious, her toes perfectly still.

'Do you hear stories then?' her uncle asked.

'Sometimes,' she said, 'and sometimes I only hear the birds singing or a bee buzzing. They're probably telling stories too, but I don't understand them.'

'Yet you understand the wind, do you?' Maren wondered.

'Oh, yes.' Mita was firm. 'The wind's stories are ones I can tell to other people.'

'And she does tell us,' her older brother spoke up. 'The stories are fun and often exciting. I don't know how she knows about the things she tells.'

Maren leaned down to the child. 'Little Mita,' he said, 'you have a very important gift. Keep listening, and if you can, teach others how to listen to the wind. The Land of Far will be lucky having you as one of its wise women.'

The wind went on telling its stories, blowing across the land and the river, rustling the leaves, bending the young trees, vibrating the bushes, making the tall grasses bow and the water skip and splash. There will always be someone to listen.

About the Author

Anne Udy is curious about people—how they relate and how they meet difficulties. She received a BA in English while in USA and married an Australian Methodist minister, with whom she worked and travelled while raising six children. She loves reading and walking. She tells herself stories when she can't get to sleep.

Printed in the United States
By Bookmasters